~~THE SKY'S THE LIMIT~~

THE STARS ARE NO LIMIT!

In a publishing coup that has already caused excitement throughout the field of speculative fiction, Pyramid Books has commissioned 4-time Hugo Winner, 2-time Nebula Winner, editor of the landmark *Dangerous Visions* anthologies, Harlan Ellison, to seek out and edit first novels by promising new talents. STORMTRACK is the first of these specially-cacheted volumes, a day-after-tomorrow adventure aboard an orbiting weather satellite, by James Sutherland, a graduate of the prestigous Clarion Writers' Workshop in SF/Fantasy.

Future titles already in work promise names such as Arthur Byron Cover and Marta Randall, names you may never have heard . . . but names that will become pleasantly familiar to readers seeking fresh views of the world of imagination. Each book bearing the words THE HARLAN ELLISON DISCOVERY SERIES is guaranteed to meet with your mind in a manner happily addictive. Quite literally, in these books, even the stars are no limit!

STORMTRACK

JAMES SUTHERLAND

PYRAMID BOOKS
NEW YORK

For Dr. Robin Scott Wilson
and Leslie Kay Swigart

STORMTRACK

A PYRAMID BOOK

Copyright © 1974, by James E. Sutherland

Introduction Copyright © 1974, by Harlan Ellison

First edition published June, 1974

ISBN 0-515-03297-2

Library of Congress Catalog Card Number: 73-21121

Printed in the United States of America

Pyramid Books are published by Pyramid Communications, Inc.
Its trademarks, consisting of the word "Pyramid" and the portrayal
of a pyramid, are registered in the United States Patent Office.

Pyramid Communications, Inc., 919 Third Avenue,
New York, New York 10022, U.S.A.

STORMTRACK

GALE WARNING

an introduction by

Harlan Ellison

I have to be careful about this. In the past I've been accused of overpromoting the writings of people with whom I've come into contact: the writers in the *Dangerous Visions* anthologies, the graduates of the Clarion Workshops in SF and fantasy, young people whose stories have impressed me. Can't deny it; I have this lemming-urge toward hyperbole. So this time I want to be cautious.

What we have here, in an inversion of the words of Strother Martin, is a success of communication.

During the summer of 1973, I was contacted by Pyramid Books in the person of their SF editor, Roger Elwood, who braced me as to the possibility of my writing a novel in collaboration with a new, unpublished writer. Apparently, because of my frequently and noisily stated commitments to supporting the unknowns in their attempts at getting published, Pyramid felt I would bite on such an offer. Wrong.

While the commitment is certainly present, it has been my experience that for every young writer one comes across who has talent and drive and a sense of craft, there are ten thousand others who think writing is as easy as learning the acoustical guitar. Wrong.

Writing itself is a difficult and exacting process, and nothing I know this side of sunbathing in a cyclotron can break a human being as quickly or thoroughly.

Writing speculative fiction only compounds the problems. It takes wit and skill and acumen and a sense of logical disorder that most people find beyond them. That it is done so well by such a small handful of people is eloquent testimony to its rigors. So I have become wary of the pathetic letters written on lined notebook paper that proclaim the manifest wonders of the communicant's talents, only awaiting to be discovered by a perceptive and patient authority like, uh, er, you, Mr. Ellison. Usually, the result is sophomoric writing and a barely concealed desire to lead the "glamorous" life of a writer. Wrong.

So I advised Pyramid that it is tough enough writing a book by oneself, that I would be a banana were I to undertake a collaboration with an untried talent. However, I said, I'd be happy to serve as general editor on a series of "first" novels under the Pyramid banner.

Thus began several months of negotiation and consideration of prospectuses that have culminated, for openers, with this first volume in what is humbly called *The Harlan Ellison Discovery Series*. Humbly? Wrong.

Quite nakedly, I'm filled with considerable pride at the publication of this book and the imminent publication of others in what I hope will prove to be a memorable series of first meetings between you . . . and them.

The "them," of course, are all the new novelists this group of books will be presenting for your judgment and support. The "you" are the readers and students of SF who have latched onto talents as various as Samuel R. Delaney, James Tiptree, Jr., Joanna Russ, Edward Bryant, Geo. Alec Effinger and others who have emerged from obscurity these last ten years and accorded them the same courtesy and support you've lavished on established writers like Asimov, Clarke, Bradbury, Herbert, Anderson, Silverberg, and even (God love you, you little weirdies) myself.

Clearly, having my name on these books is a marketing device. Where you might be loath to lay out the cover price for a novel by someone whose name is unknown to you, I've made enough noise and trouble these last few years that your morbid curiosity may be piqued by a book "discovered" by me. So in one of the few viable ways an established writer who has reaped the benefits proffered by the SF field can pay back some of that kindness, I have set myself up in this series as a Judas goat, a stalking horse, a figurehead, if you will, and, trading on whatever points I've made with you personally, use that nebulous liaison to get you to listen to the throaty rumblings of some young tigers.

The books in this series will be of all sorts. There will be hard science novels, like this one . . . experimental novels such as ones now under consideration by Arthur Byron Cover and Marta Randall . . . fantasies . . . novels of characterization in SF . . . uncategorizables . . .

But each of them will have been selected by, packaged by, edited by, and hustled by your not-so-humble servant. Few, if any, will be the sort of books I would choose to write myself. (For instance, *this* book is extrapolative hard science, a kind of story God knows *I've* never been accused of having written. It is closely reasoned, well-researched, and almost entirely devoid of the insane emotional assaults my own work leans on so heavily.) But they will be books I've enjoyed reading, by talented newcomers whom I feel deserve a showcase and a fair chance in the overcrowded marketplace. If I don't thrill you with one selection, try another, I urge you . . . there will be enough strange dishes in this long banquet of discoveries to satisfy even the most jaded of appetites.

Nepotism is an ugly word. Let's just say that I've been watching the career of James Sutherland very closely since I first met him at a Clarion Workshop in Pennsylvania in 1968. That he has been in and out of Ellison Wonderland for the past few years is a matter it ill concerns you to consider. We are not related. But when you're planning a series of first novels and a good one is lying on the desk in the guest room, having just come back from an authority as unimpeachable as Ben

Bova of *Analog* with rave reactions, you'd be a nerd not to slither in, grab it, and dash for the goal line.

Yes, Sutherland is a friend, but if you can't publish the good work of your friends, as opposed to the crap of strangers, what's the point of *having* an open house for bright talents?

In any case (having cleverly extricated myself from any Watergatian inferences of corruption), Jim is twenty-five years old as this is written. He was born on August 25, 1948 in Greenwich, Connecticut, offspring of talented parents (father a full professor of Graphic Arts at Rochester Institute of Technology, mother a health teacher at a Rochester high school), a strapping youth with regular features and an appetite that has contributed heavily to the food crisis in this country.

After brief stays in West Virginia and New York City, the Sutherland family settled in Rochester where Jim attended RIT, emerging with a Bachelor of Science degree. After attending the University of Buffalo, he was one of the most outstanding writers to come out of the early Clarion Workshops of which he attended two, in 1968 and 1969.

His first sale was to the omnipresent David Gerrold, for his anthology of new writings, *Generation.* Sale made in 1970. Since that time he has placed almost two dozen stories and articles with markets as varied as *Vertex, Rolling Stone, The Magazine of Fantasy & Science Fiction* and several original anthologies, not the least of which is *The Last Dangerous Visions* (which I would be a nut not to mention). I urge you not to miss his brilliant contribution to that monumental volume. It is titled "The Amazonas Link" and is a *terrific* piece of writing. Look for it next year.

At the moment he is living in Long Beach, California, keeping company with the incredibly memorable Leslie Kay Swigart, and furiously writing a second novel, dealing with ESP.

His interest in, and familiarity with, the physical sciences has made him a recognizable voice in the field of science nonfiction articles and nowhere does that talent demonstrate itself to more advantage than here in STORMTRACK, his first full-length work.

Stormtrack has a young protagonist, but it is not what is termed in the publishing industry a "juvenile." It is a mature, fully realized novel of technological extrapolation. The youth of its protagonist, Ross Moran, speaks directly to the fascination of many young writers in the SF genre with people of their own age. Heretofore in SF, it was *de rigueur* to make the viewpoint character a man, about thirty, whole in all his parts, keen-eyed, attractive, and if possible a technical engineer capable of creating a hyperspace drive from six safety pins and a cardboard tube from the toilet paper roll. Things have changed in the field, happily, and while we still have our share of Hawk Carses and Kimball Kinnisons and Captain Futures, there is now room for "heroes" like Ross Moran, who happens to be a young person, just like many of you, no matter what your age or sex or educational background.

Stormtrack is concerned with the unfolding character of Moran, of course, but as with the best of all SF, the background and society play a dominant role.

The satellite station *Boreas* is a character (and a damned intriguing one at that); the crowded, troubled world of 1996 with its tipsy cooperation between major powers is also a major character. And against that technological and sociological background Jim Sutherland has laid a fascinating and complex story of double-dealing, espionage, and danger. Sutherland has even plotted a sting in the tail of this novel that will both surprise and satisfy you.

As Ben Bova says of this book, "Although some science fiction readers wonder if there is anything new for SF writers to tackle, the truth is that there are many subject areas that are of enormous intrinsic interest and are virtually untapped, as far as story material is concerned. Jim Sutherland has zeroed in on one of these areas, weather monitoring and control. With clarity and

11

accurate technological extrapolation, he presents a vivid picture of why weather monitoring and modification will be of vital importance in the very near future, and how this vital task can be accomplished."

As Ellison says of the first novel in this series—one that will hopefully drag you back for the second and third and subsequent revelations—what we have here is a storm warning of great disorders to come. Burgeoning talents, fresh on the scene, hopping up and down to get you to read *their* dangerous visions. What we have here is an exciting story, written directly and with considerable inventiveness, as a banner blowing in the wind of change the SF field has felt this last decade. It's a gale warning, and I invite you to step into the fresh air and let the winds ruffle your imaginations.

HARLAN ELLISON
Los Angeles
January 30, 1974

CHAPTER ONE

In the heat of the morning the city moved.

As he stepped from the monorail he saw it. Currents of dusty pavement heat made the buildings waver and heave like a row of exhausted animals panting in the sun. Across the street, the Government Center towered over them, reminding Ross why he had just traveled all the way here. He had no choice, once a week *they* required him to report in.

It's the same as parole, Ross thought, as he watched the Center building pulsate slowly. Except—I'm not a criminal, am I?

He glanced at his watch. Two minutes.

He was going to have to hurry, as usual, or miss his scheduled "consultation" with the computer, and that would never, never do. Pushing through the crowd around the main door, Ross wondered what would happen if he decided to skip a week, or if the monorail broke down, or if he got that new flu going around. But he knew the answer. He would promptly lose his job. Or rather his nonjob.

Better get a move on, he told himself.

The Weather Service maintained a suite of offices on the Center's ground floor. Ross ducked through the crowded lobby and walked into the personnel office. He looked around. It was a familiar scene.

Queues of hopeful job-seekers looped along the walls of the office. Applicants who had been turned down stood in the center of the room with sullen looks on their faces. Both groups eyed Ross suspiciously as he briskly crossed the floor and stopped before the head secretary's desk. Ross knew what they were thinking: what's so special about *that* kid that he doesn't have to stand in line like the rest of us?

Ross wished he could tell them. Nothing special. Nothing at all. He looked down uncomfortably.

The head secretary of the personnel office had been replaced temporarily by an attractive, businesslike young woman who took Ross's ID card and made a notation that he had kept his appointment. Then, holding his card in one hand, she checked it against a typed list of recent Service hirings.

In spite of himself, Ross felt his heart beat faster. It was ridiculous to get excited, he said to himself. Every week you report in, and every week you receive the same response. Zero. Why should this week, this day, be different than the two dozen preceding? No reason, yet he was trembling excitedly as the woman behind the desk put down her list and leveled her gaze at him.

"I'm sorry, Mr. Moran," she told him. "There are no changes in the hiring schedule." She returned his card and gave him a look of professional sympathy.

Ross handed the card right back.

"Would you mind rechecking, please?" he said, hoping the sudden burst of desperation he felt now didn't emerge in his voice.

"Well." She paused, and then replied, "Sure. No problem," and inserted the ID into a desktop computer console that was tied into the main data bank at Weather Service headquarters in Washington. The machine would cross-search the records and determine in seconds whether Ross's employment status had changed. There always was a slight chance that the Service had decided to employ him, but had not transmitted the order to this branch.

Ross noticed that the secretary was studying his face intently.

"Moran . . . Moran," she repeated in a whisper, as though she imagined the name might spark an elusive memory. Her eyes seemed to brighten and she said, "Of course! Two years back I dated a guy named Moran. You know, you look a lot like him, his height, same dark hair, the same eyes. He was in the Service too—a pilot."

Ross stirred uneasily. "Do you remember his name?"

"Hmm. Sam," the girl said, smiling, after a moment. "Sam Moran. Any relation?"

"Yes. He was my brother."

"Was?" The girl looked at him curiously.

"Sam was killed last July, near Guam."

The smile vanished. "Oh. I'm terribly sorry, I didn't know," she said awkwardly. Then a print-out began emerging from the computer:

UNITED STATES WEATHER SERVICE
Washington, D.C.

Ross skimmed down past the form number, the lines containing his Los Angeles address, and the entry of his twenty-second birthdate to his work record file.

Damn! Not an item was changed. It still read:

```
Applicant status:      Hired
Wage rate:             Subsistence
Occupational level:    Hold
```

Ross groaned in disappointment, then turned to the secretary and said, "Thanks for querying. You were right."

"We'll let you know if anything develops," she replied faintly.

Ross nodded and strode on out of the Center. Moments later he was standing on the sidewalk. People went rushing by him on their way to work and Ross felt a sudden pang of envy watching them surge past. All the thousands of faces in that stream of humanity possessed a special quality Ross wished he had also.

They all seem to know who they are and where they are going, he thought. They're not simply drifting along. Drifting. . . .

He started walking in no particular direction now. With his one obligation of this day and week finished the remainder of the morning and afternoon was free and empty.

He was near the entrance to the downtown monorail terminal when a hollow-eyed teenage girl approached him and pleaded for money. Wordlessly, Ross gave her his last dollar bill and she slipped back into the crowd.

After going on a little further, Ross shrugged his shoulders and retraced his steps and boarded an express for the San Fernando Valley. The monorail coach was old and dusty and crammed full with exhausted office workers heading for home after the night shift. There was no place to sit and barely enough time to grab for a stanchion before the train lurched forward. Ross held on tightly as other commuters, less wary and rested, stumbled against him and mumbled apologies.

He hardly noticed them. He ignored the cityscape flowing across the grime-streaked windows.

His thoughts kept returning to the Weather Service office. The scene became bright and sharp again in his memory, and he found the brief conversation replaying itself over and over.

"I'm sorry Mr. Moran. There are no changes in the hiring schedule, the secretary repeated endlessly.

Would you mind rechecking, please?

Sure. No problem.

No problem at all, Ross thought bitterly. No problem if you have a steady job, your own place and freedom. But it *is* a problem if you're stuck with a *hold* on your life and you live with relatives who tolerate you only because they need that room and board money for their own kids. Ross felt queasy as the monorail floated around a curve at high speed.

Sure. No problem.

The sick, giddy feeling refused to go away as the train descended among the twisting Hollywood Hills, and then roared through the valley flatlands. When it began to brake for the first station, Ross realized he had neither the desire nor the strength to return home. He couldn't face that stagnant little houseful of screaming children and their sullen, resentful parents.

Got to get out—away from all these people, he told himself. Got to find some green quiet place, sit down, and think about where I'm going.

It took several minutes to thread his way to the exit, but soon Ross was off the monorail and looking eagerly for the escalator that would carry him to the ground floor of this station.

Something stopped him between steps.

He went to the edge of the platform. Pressed against the guard railing, he saw the enormous city that filled the San Fernando Valley from rim to rim. A layer of yellowish haze spotted sections of the patchwork community, but here and there gleaming towers pushed through the smog like immense metal flowers reaching for the October sunlight. A helicopter banked in the overcast and settled to a landing atop one of the office buildings.

Beyond it, the city continued to unroll before his eyes like a glittering map.

Almost against his will, Ross started searching for the houses and the streets, the parks and stores and the neighborhoods where he had lived most of his life.

Over there, buried in urban Van Nuys was the old high school Ross and his brother had attended. Somewhere nearby was the house—or had that whole block been demolished for a Mall? He couldn't remember.

Nothing there made any sense.

It's a huge anthill, he thought wildly. And there's no escape—it keeps going on and on and on. . . .

"Hey! 'Scuse me, bud," a burly workman growled, shoving past Ross. Like cold water splashed on his face,

17

the words jarred him. They cleared his head and let him think.

Wait a minute! There is a place out there, he thought after a moment. There is a quiet place and green.

He began walking for the bus loop.

For some inexplicable reason it was named Fernvale, though no ferns had ever grown there and it was hardly more than a notch in the hillside.

The sun that blazed down on the cemetery all day, drying the grass a shade browner and heating the marker stones until they were warm to the touch, had long ago reached the zenith. Now it was fast settling toward a shelf of low clouds. Ross felt his fingers tremble when he touched the smooth marble that marked his brother's grave.

He let his eyes wander to the freshly chiseled name:

Samuel W. Moran
1971—1995

Ross leaned against a sedate Dutch elm that spread cool dappled shadows over the grassy plot.

This was a peaceful spot, familiar and nearly friendly. Every few weeks Ross took the bus here, occasionally to avoid the smog and heat, sometimes to escape the confines of his room. But mostly to be near Sammy again.

He recalled there had been a time—it was directly after the funeral—when the cemetery seemed to be a morbid and forbidding place. Ross had to work up his courage even to think of going, and when he did he always brought along geraniums and asters to placate his subtle fear. During the summer his feelings changed. His anxiety evaporated and he discarded the flower ritual; geraniums and asters weren't Sammy's style, he decided one day.

He sat beside a gnarled root.

Well, Sammy, that's the fourth time this month I've

been turned down at that damn office, Ross thought.

What do I do?

A breeze lifted the brown grass slightly.

This *Hold* business is sending me up the wall, Sammy. No way out of it, either. I never should have signed that agreement.

Ross smiled ruefully, remembering his brother's advice. It had been at Ross's graduation from Caltech five months ago. Sammy had warned Ross not to accept the Weather Service contract, telling him about his own experiences with the Service.

Sammy didn't know that out of a hundred in Ross's class, only a dozen had received employment offers. Nobody, it seemed, wanted meteorologists—there were far too many graduates for the number of available jobs. You either snapped at an offer, *any* offer, or you waited around for years probably until another offer came along.

Ross didn't want to wait. He signed. The Weather Service gave him a fine talk, a miniscule salary, and entered his name on a list of those to get a full job when their turn came.

Weeks, months had gone by, nearly half a year. Still no word.

As always, the silent grave echoed his thoughts, and for a moment Ross was drawn from his own situation. He stared at the new gravestone and wondered as he had a hundred times: what was the end like, Sammy?

He'd heard only the sketchiest details. A fierce tropical typhoon had approached Guam Island in the Central Pacific. The Weather Service, concerned whether the storm would strike Guam, sent out a venerable search plane with special radars and forecasting computers; Sammy flew into the typhoon.

The jet suffered something called "explosive decompression": the fuselage came apart in flight and the debris fell into the eye of the hurricane.

After the storm veered away, Air-Sea Rescue found the body.

That was all Ross knew about it, though his dreams

19

were haunted by a searing image of those final seconds aloft: an impossible wind, then fire and flashes of pain and falling. Falling forever.

The sun was setting and the streetlights were flickering on when the bus halted and left Ross at the corner opposite his aunt and uncle's house.

He expected to hear the kids yowling or running in the yard. Long ago Aunt Louise had given up anything but a pretense of keeping them in hand, since the nearest playground was a mile away.

Tonight the house was strangely quiet, and Ross went up the front steps with some trepidation, wondering what was wrong. Maybe one of the kids broke an arm; maybe Uncle Herbert got fired from the recycling plant. Maybe both. He opened the door.

Aunt Louise was in the hallway, filling a bowl with cheap candy. She looked up in surprise. "Oh, it's you. Where've you been?"

"Wandering around."

"While you were out this arrived," she said and gave him a small parcel. It was wrapped tightly. Ross had to use both hands to break the sealing tape webbed about a flat object the size and shape of a pack of playing cards.

"It's Sammy's flashlight!" said Ross, stunned, turning it over in his hand and seeing the initials S.W.M. engraved on the dented aluminum casing.

Louise nodded rapidly. "The man that delivered it said it washed ashore on Guam last week. It was floating all that time. Imagine!"

Ross held the flashlight numbly. *Sammy!*

He hardly heard something pattering up the porch steps outside, or the giggling. But when the door chimes rang it was like an explosion. He whirled and swung the door open.

"Trick or treat," called three children in unison. They were dressed in bright garish costumes and held out paper sacks to Ross. "Trick or treat, mister?" one repeated hopefully.

Ross's aunt edged past him and distributed candy from the bowl. "Going to be like this for hours more," she said wearily. "You better not count on getting to sleep early."

"I didn't realize today was Halloween," replied Ross. "I hope they enjoy themselves."

"They will. Ours took off an hour ago. We saved some supper for you."

Ross slipped the flashlight into his jacket pocket, followed his aunt to the kitchen table, and sat down across from his dour uncle Herbert who was reading the paper. Louise set a bowl of clamless chowder in front of Ross. That—and Halloween—was a sure sign of the end of October: the government rationed fish and meat on the middle and last days of each month.

This also was the day his room and board came due, a subject Herbert broached early in the meal.

"Can I pay you tomorrow?" Ross said slowly.

"I guess it's OK. You start working tomorrow?"

"No. I'm still classified *Hold*."

Instantly Ross regretted the admission. His fruitless trips to the Weather Service office always seemed to provoke his relatives to ask, had Ross finally gotten his job? His denial would bring another question, often caustic, sometimes bitter. Around and around it would go until everybody was hurt. Ross was sure nobody planned it that way. One spark would lead to another and then another, and before any of them realized what was happening the smoldering resentment would bloom into an angry fire.

"I still don't understand why a strong, intelligent boy like you isn't already hired," Louise said.

That *"boy"* stung.

"I am hired," Ross told her, trying to rein in his temper. "We've been through this bit a thousand times and I—"

"But you're not working. You say that you're hired, but you sit around the house all the time," Herbert said, laying down his paper.

21

Well folks, here we go again! The debate of the decade! Ross thought.

"The Weather Service has classified me *Hold*," he said patiently. "the same as dozens of other guys. All the jobs get rotated among us; when there's one for me I'll be notified. That's what the secretary said today."

"Did she also tell you the government doesn't know its bean from a teakettle?" said Herbert. "They'll make you sit on your duff forever, Ross. You ought to sign up with a private outfit. An airline or something."

"I've already signed on with the Weather Service. For a five-year contract beginning the day after graduation. There's a clause that states side deals are out. Out!

"Look," Ross continued, pleading, "let's skip the subject. My room money gets paid on time. What more do you want?"

More money—that's what they wanted. Ross knew that as soon as his salary increased, so would his living expenses. And he couldn't move out for a while; the Housing Control Board had a nine-month wait for apartments in Southern California.

"Oh, Ross," sighed Louise. "We're both concerned about your welfare." Ross barely disguised a snort of disgust. Louise, looking miffed and unappreciated, continued, "I promised your mother, just before she, she—"

Louise stammered a trifle. She paused, then lifted her head slightly.

"Before she passed on, I promised her I would care for you and Samuel and keep you out of trouble and see that you went to college—"

The conversation lapsed awkwardly.

Herbert was staring at Ross with what he assumed was suspicion.

"Did you really go down to that office today? Or just call 'em up and then go roaming around?" he asked Ross in a low voice. He shook his head. "I simply don't know. You're always at loose ends nowadays. Times like this I despair that you'll ever change."

Thanks for the vote of confidence, Ross thought. Just what the doctor required to top off a lovely day.

Ross looked away, angrier at himself than at his aunt and uncle. I should have kept quiet!

Herbert rattled on awhile as Louise stacked the dirty tureens and silverware and dumped them into the dishwasher.

The tension broke.

With a shattering *clang!* the door chimes pealed. Herbert and Louise exchanged looks, then Herbert rose from his chair and stalked away.

He returned pale and shaken.

"What's the matter, dear?" Louise glanced at the door. "Those kids, did they—"

Herbert shook his head no.

"There's a man at the door, he wants to speak to you, Ross."

"The Weather Service?" said Ross wonderingly. It was so late in the day for the call to come.

His voice sounding weak and small and very distant, Herbert replied, "Nothing like that. He's from the FBI."

CHAPTER TWO

Agent Daniel Webster Carmichael of the Federal Bureau of Investigation leveled his gaze at Ross.

"You," he said, "are pretty good—for an amateur. That was a nice slip you gave me on the monorail. I missed seeing it until I got all the way to Van Nuys. Spent the rest of the day trying to backtrack."

In the dim lamplight of the front porch, he was every bit the traditional "special operative" Ross had seen in countless movies: middleaged, yet rugged and lean in a charcoal gray suit. Carmichael was wearing a conspicuous pistol holster on his belt that remained completely steady when he moved down the steps.

"No matter. You're here now."

He reached inside his jacket, and for the slightest moment Ross feared Carmichael was going for his gun. Instead, the agent produced a large manila envelope which he gave to Ross without comment and stepped back.

Ross pulled the tab at one end and a sheaf of papers dropped into his lap. On the top was a document embossed with an official-looking seal and covered with typescript, signed and countersigned. Next was a letter. The light was not good enough to make out what it said in detail, but it was headed by massive block capitals spelling out UNITED STATES OF AMERI-

CA: AUTHORIZATION FOR TRANSFER AND RELOCATION OF PERSONNEL, followed by the word *Expedite* in a bold hand.

Ross whistled. "Most impressive. Am I under arrest?"

"Not unless you willfully obstruct the provisions of the authorization," Carmichael told him.

"What happens then"

"I file for a federal court order to enforce the authorization, Mr. Moran. Either way you're coming with me."

"I see," said Ross heavily. "Well then, where?"

Carmichael shrugged his shoulders. "You've got the traveling papers, not me. All I am supposed to say is this. Please settle your affairs here and pack up your belongings. Leave the driving to me," said Carmichael, smiling slightly.

"It appears I don't have much choice in this," Ross said.

"I suppose not."

Ross sat back until his shoulder blades touched the door frame, considering what to do. It all seemed so confusing and muddled, and yet, really, he had only to decide between two alternatives. Very simply he could go with Carmichael or obstinately remain here in this house for—how long? How long would it require for Carmichael to pry a court order out? Not long, Ross guessed.

He got up. "All right."

A minute later he was tossing his clothes into a pair of scuffed and battered suitcases. Shirts, sweaters, his old suit and shoes and socks, then a few books and his razor. That was all. Ross was surprised to see how little he had and how quickly it could be stowed. He carried the suitcases downstairs.

Carmichael was talking to Ross's aunt, Herbert was reading the authorization intently. Neither of them had much to say to him.

Carmichael put the bags into the trunk of a powerful

turbine cruiser parked at the curb and slammed shut the trunk lid while Louise and Herbert said goodbye in strained, uncertain voices. Ross promised he'd write them.

They waved as the cruiser growled away, bearing Ross and Carmichael toward the southbound freeway entrance.

"Nice people," said Carmichael, looking in the mirror.

Ross nodded, vague thoughts crowding his mind. "I wonder when I'll see them again?" he said, looking at Carmichael.

"If you're asking me where you're headed, I'll be honest; I don't know. I'm just driving you to the airport, that's all."

Trucks and other cars went whirling by as the cruiser accelerated southward through the city.

"But why? Why me?" Ross asked later.

"Who knows?"

"What are you hiding?" Ross demanded. "What's gone wrong?"

Carmichael turned in his seat. "Believe me, I don't know; they didn't tell me much about you, or what you were into. You see the word *Expedite?* Well, that's what I'm supposed to be doing. Expediting. Here's the airport."

The car swung down an exit ramp.

Frowning, Ross unsealed the document package again and began leafing through its contents, searching for a clue to his destination, his situation, anything. Near the bottom of the stack of unreadable legal forms was a computerized airline ticket and reservation. It was issued by an obscure outfit, something named Transit Lines, Inc., which Ross guessed was either a small local outfit or one of those nebulous charter lines that operated out of a broom closet. He was about to look further when he saw the price mark. His eyes widened.

"Thirty-seven hundred and sixty dollars," he said, gasping.

Carmichael grunted in appreciation. "You must be a VIP, Mr. Moran. Guess I had better call you *sir* from here on!"

"Don't bother. Just tell me where a $3760.00 ticket would take someone."

"Further than I'm going," replied Carmichael, heading the car through a maze of lanes and exits. He slowed the cruiser gradually, finally leaving it parked beneath a curved portico. Ross saw a small baggage stand and an equally diminutive ticket counter inside with the words *Transit Lines* emblazoned across the front.

Carmichael handed over Ross's luggage to a porter, validated the ticket and rushed Ross to a waiting elevator before Ross had the chance to scan the arrival-and-departure board for a hint of his flight's destination. Once in the elevator, the FBI man glanced at his watch with a worried frown.

"You're late," Carmichael said. "Just hope they haven't pulled back the ramp."

The elevator doors hissed open, and Ross saw Carmichael smile.

"Made it," he said to Ross. "There's your transportation. Well, this is as far as I go. Luck." He shook Ross's hand briskly and walked back to the elevators. A flight attendant escorted Ross to the ramp gate, and from a window that opened out onto the concrete aprons and runways Ross caught a glimpse of his "transportation." It was huge and white, with stubby wings that were almost fins and enormous engine exhausts that poked from the tail like a battery of heavy artillery.

From the ramp gate, a moving walkway carried him inside. A hatch closed behind him with a muffled thud. Ross blinked in surprise.

Judging from its outsize dimensions, Ross had supposed the interior would have been cavernous, filled with many hundreds of seats. Instead, the cabin was as cramped and constricted as the inside of a tube of toothpaste. Altogether it consisted of only a pair of double seat rows flanking an aisle so narrow he had to sidle down it. He found, at last, an unoccupied aisle seat, dropped his coat onto it, and started to sit down.

"Hello!" a voice said. "Sorry, but I'm sitting there."

Ross turned his head.

The voice belonged to a girl standing next to him.

Ross saw an oval face framed with styled blonde hair, saw her dress of ultramarine and white velour, saw the silver belt circling her trim waist. Last of all he saw beautiful deep gray eyes looking right into his.

The adjacent seat, beside a thick triple-paned observation window, was untaken; Ross transferred himself and his coat there. Gracefully the girl seated herself.

Ross leaned back into the lush foam cushions, thinking, this could be a delightful flight, indeed.

Wherever it was destined.

"Thank you," she said, her voice softer. "Is this your first trip up?" She placed an odd emphasis on the final word in her question.

Ross's eyes darted to her. "No, I've flown several times," he replied. It seemed to reassure her slightly, but he could still discern tension lining her next words.

"Oh. I never have." She smiled nervously and her gaze seemed to criss-cross the space between Ross and the window several times. "It's supposed to be beautiful—the view."

Ross nodded vaguely. The view of *what?*

"Tell me, what does it really look like?"

His thoughts interrupted, Ross looked quizzically at her.

"You know," she said insistently. "Main Station."

"Main Station?" For the second time in a minute Ross frowned, puzzled. "I never heard of the place."

The girl twisted, staring at him with round eyes. "You *are* joking."

The plane started rolling and the motion seemed to jog loose a nearly forgotten scrap of a memory from

28

an old newscast. Main Station. Ross shut his eyes tightly.

Main Station.

The pieces all began to fall together, so that it was unnecessary for the stewardess to announce a minute later, "Welcome to Transit Lines Flight Four. We will be docking at the Main Space Station in fifty-seven minutes."

Of course, Ross thought.

The space shuttle plane went screaming down the runway.

Two hundred miles above the coast of Spain the shuttle's engine shut down on schedule, and Flight Four began its long drift toward rendezvous at 17,400 miles per hour.

The crushing weight Ross had felt vanished utterly with the last rumbling of the rockets; instantly the same giddy feeling he had experienced on the monorail many hours ago returned with a vengeance. He wondered how his friend one seat over was taking it. Quite well, it seemed.

She was eagerly looking out the window set in the cabin wall beside Ross's seat.

"There's Orion and Gemini," she said enthusiastically. "It's lovely. Say, you're awfully pale. If you loosen the restraining straps the weightlessness isn't so bad."

He tried it. "Thanks," he said gratefully.

"Don't mention it. If you develop a headache from the cabin pressure changes later on I've got a couple of aspirins left."

"You're well equipped."

"I'll take that as a compliment," she said lightly. "But really it is part of my business. I'm going to be working with the medical staff on Main Station."

"Nurse?" Ross inquired.

"Heavens, no," she said, sounding a trifle insulted by the suggestion. "I'll be doing research into the effect of weightlessness on heart disease."

29

"Could I have one of those aspirins? My head's buzzing."

She placed a white pill in his hand and closed his fingers around it. "I'll ring the stewardess for a bulb of water."

In a while the buzzing diminished. The shuttle had overhauled Main Station and was matching orbits prior to docking; tiny vernier control jets added a slow wing-over wing roll to the shuttle, duplicating the rotation of the wheel-shaped station's hub.

The faint sensation of weight was returning as the primary thrusters nudged the shuttle toward the gaping hub. As Flight Four neared the station Ross could discern more details of the vast spider web of metal and transparent plastic turning against the black sky.

"Thirty seconds to docking," the pilot reported.

With infinite caution the shuttle inched forward, shuddering delicately with each correction thrust of the verniers. Ross craned his neck to see a featureless expanse of aluminum occupying the entire window; it was a glittering arch moving majestically in an endless circle.

"Ten seconds."

From the hub walls three servo-equipped magnetic arms swung out to position the shuttle.

A flexible entryway descended upon the shuttle's hatch like a lamprey. Ross could hear locking bolts slamming home like hammers thudding invisibly all around him.

The hatch slid back and a gust of new strange-smelling air blew into the cabin. There was the slightest tinge of ozone and machine oil in it, and the scent of green living things.

"Docking is complete," the pilot announced. "Passengers may unlatch their belts and prepare to disembark via the center hatch.

Ross looked at the convoluted steel beams and braces along the walls of the station hub and thought, can this be it? This is my final destination?

The passengers now were stirring, gathering up their possessions and making their way to the middle of the shuttle. It was like a signal.

Transit Lines Flight Four—Los Angeles Metro Airport to the International Space Administration's Main Station in Earth orbit—was completed.

CHAPTER THREE

"You are Mr. Ross Moran?"

Ross nodded at the uniformed aide who stood impassively at the end of the exit from the shuttle. "That's right."

"If you will come with me, sir. I have already arranged for your luggage to be stored temporarily. This way, please."

Ross found he was by this time too exhausted to argue or even question. He yawned, following the aide into an elevator. It descended from the hub to the rim of the station in a single extended motion; all the way Ross felt his weight begin to ebb back until, by the moment the door opened again, it seemed normal.

Main Station was unlike anything Ross had ever imagined. Utterly clean throughout and staffed with alert men and women, it still projected an informal, easy-going ambiance. And yet there was also an undeniable air of self-confidence. Ross found it a simple matter to forget that he was nine hundred miles above the last wispy traces of the Earth's atmosphere, and to imagine he was strolling through one of the hopeful New Cities in Canada or South America.

They passed a row of shops and restaurants, arriving at the paneled office marked by a brass plate: D. K.

Gurvich, Director of Operations, ISA. The aide departed. A stout middle-aged man stood up from behind his desk and extended his hand in greeting the moment the door resealed shut.

"Mr. Moran? I am pleased to meet you. My name is Dimitri Gurvich." He pumped Ross's arm and smiled vigorously.

"Glad to meet you," Ross replied. "I suppose you're the man I can thank for this excursion."

The smile vanished from Gurvich's face, and he motioned Ross to take a seat beside the desk.

"In a way, yes," Gurvich said slowly, his Russian accent making each word seem thick and heavy. "I wish to extend my apologies for the abrupt manner by which you were brought to Main Station, and I realize you have every right to be angry. The past few hours must have been—ah—unsettling."

"You might say that."

"Please believe that I have the greatest repugnance and distaste for the entire operation, Mr. Moran, even though I believe it was justified in principle."

Ross doubted it and said as much.

"Allow me to explain my situation," Gurvich said. "Only twenty hours ago I was forced to locate an immediate replacement for a meteorologist aboard one of our weather-observation satellites. There simply wasn't time to go through the usual processes—going through the files, advertising, that kind of thing—so I called upon an old friend and explained my need for someone both young and intelligent, and someone possessing the requisite background and skills, of course."

The man fixed Ross with a cool, steady gaze and added, "he recommended you. So far I am inclined to agree with him."

Ross nodded, then, feeling a trifle wary, asked who his benefactor was.

"An instructor of yours at your university. He prefers to remain anonymous."

"So now I'm David Copperfield," Ross muttered,

shaking his head. "All right then, why this secrecy—the FBI and so forth?"

"Of that I had no part," Gurvich replied defensively. "My superiors in the ISA demanded it."

"But there was no reason."

"I agree with you, and yet—" Gurvich's voice faded slightly. He stopped and looked searchingly again at Ross. "Let me put the problem to you as they did to me. Each day the world becomes more crowded, and each day there is less food to go around. Until now famine has been averted largely by a network of observers on the Earth and here in orbit, to keep a close watch on the weather and indicate its effect on agricultural production. Without this data long-range planning is impossible, and mass starvation threatens. Everything interlocks and is so very delicate, like a house made of straws. Remove one piece, even a tiny one, and the house tumbles.

"At this moment such a weak point exists. It is on the observation satellite, and I *must* shore it up quickly," Gurvich said.

"You've picked the wrong person," Ross said in protest. "I'm no expert. In fact, I'm just out of college. Did your friend tell you I don't have any experience?"

Gurvich waved that away, saying, "Experience is not the deciding factor. You can acquire whatever you may have missed in short order. I know by your record that you're adept with machinery. But you have an even more desirable quality; you can adapt. You coped well with the rapid chain of events that brought you here, if a bit unwillingly."

"I'll agree to that last phrase."

"Then perhaps you may be imagining that this was a stunt. Let me assure you, Mr. Moran, that it was not. It was a test."

"A test?"

"Precisely," Gurvich said, standing up once again. "You have passed it. I believe you will be a fine member of the satellite crew, but of course the choice is yours. Take whatever time you need to reach a decision. You might enjoy seeing more of Main Station, to get acquainted with living conditions in orbit."

Ross was bone-tired, but he assented, feeling his native curiosity taking control.

"Fine. I have the perfect guide for you," said Gurvich, summoning a tall, well-dressed young man with shaggy light brown hair and a pair of piercing blue eyes shining behind wire-rimmed glasses. The director made the introductions, and Ross learned that the newcomer was one Timothy Diehle, MD.

"Welcome to Main Station," he said in greeting, and grinned. "Did Dimitri just pass judgment on your fate?"

"Doctor," Gurvich said firmly, "will you please escort Mr. Moran wherever he desires and answer his questions about *Boreas*."

"*Boreas*. What's that?"

"What everybody calls the weather station," Ross's guide said, heading for the door. "Boreas was the Greek god of the north wind, and since the observation is primarily devoted to the arctic, the name seemed appropriate."

"Is Boreas as large as Main Station, Doctor?" Ross asked, as they entered a wide corridor flanked by storage bays.

"Much smaller, but there're only twelve in the crew altogether, so it evens out," was the reply. "Incidently, despite the impression our director may have given you, most everybody here goes on a first name basis. Too little room, otherwise!"

"You work on *Boreas,* then?"

Tim nodded. "This is just shore leave for me."

Gradually he filled Ross with a description of the little community of *Boreas* station that daily orbited out some twenty-six thousand miles from Earth, and then swung back to within a mere two thousand. "It's lonely sometimes," Tim said. "*Boreas* has its drawbacks, but it's still a pretty fair place to go to get away from the Earth."

"You don't mean that, do you?" said Ross, startled.

"Why not?" Tim said, suddenly thoughtful. He halted and indicated the view from a vast transparent panel that was one of the station walls: a sliver of the world bathed in sunlight and glowing green and turquoise and streaked with ivory.

"From here it's all a wonderful sight—cities and oceans and clouds. But when you go down there and see it the way it actually is! The clouds are dirty smoke, the seas are foul with oil and sewage, and the cities! They're jungles, most of them."

Tim gazed sadly outward. "Until two years ago, when I started work on *Boreas,* I never actually realized how well people have succeeded in wrecking the Earth. Now I don't care if I never return there. I'm beginning to like space, it's the only place they've not spoiled."

Ross heard those phrases and those emotions echoed by many others later, the men and women who called the orbital stations, shuttles, and space tugs home. It was a bitter renunciation of their birthplace, and a long-shot bet that technology and their own wits and spirits could keep them alive and give their lives meaning.

"I wonder sometimes," said Tim, "if one morning I'll hear that all life on Earth has been erased by a catastrophe. Then only the people on the satellites would be around to carry on, and that scares me." He turned from the glass wall. "Come on, there's a person I want you to meet."

They entered the rear of a crowded, smoke-congested auditorium that sloped downward to a dais where a man was rapping his gavel and calling for order. Above his head was stretched a long paper banner; Welcome! Congress of Radio Astronomers.

The gavel banged again, louder.

"Sirs and ladies!" the figure behind the dais shouted. "Take your places, please. All of you have been on Main Station long enough to know you can't float away!"

"That's Dr. Alfred Nystrom," Tim said, waving toward the platform, and despite the murk and turmoil the wave was recognized and returned. "He's the resident astronomer on *Boreas*," Tim told Ross over the incredible din, "and first speaker for the convention. He's in for a rough time—few of the delegates have even been aboard a space station before. They're pretty excited!"

The delegates cleared the aisles and were finding their seats, and Ross took a close look at the figure now launching into his speech. Dr. Nystrom appeared to be well into his fifties and was nearly bald, but he had a massive frame and a strong voice and a likeable persistence with his fellow scientists, who were settling down now to listen. Ross recognized a few of the faces in the audience from the shuttle flight up from Los Angeles.

Tim nudged Ross, saying, "There's an—ah—errand I have to see to. Be back in a minute."

Ross hardly heard him leave. Drowsing in his comfortable chair with his eyes half-closed, Ross caught snatches of the speech. The minute Tim had promised lengthened to twenty, and then the speech was over and applause broke from the audience.

Ross tried to rouse himself when he glanced about and saw the delegates heading for the doorways, chattering among themselves. Tim was nowhere in the auditorium.

So much for the guided tour, Ross thought, getting to his feet and stretching his arms wide.

Dr. Alfred Nystrom came walking up to Ross, accompanied by a slight Oriental. He cheerfully introduced himself, and then his companion, "My old friend, Dr. Ahn Il Kim. Used to teach at the University of Korea, but the U.S. Air Force has him now, slaving away in Denver on something or other *very* classified."

They all shook hands, then Dr. Nystrom asked if Ross had had lunch yet.

"I don't remember finishing supper," Ross said.

"Join us then? Delivering speeches gives me a fear-

37

some appetite, and besides, you haven't lived until you've eaten a Main Station meal. Don't worry about Tim. He'll find us." He led them out of the empty auditorium to a nearby restaurant decorated like a Paris cafe. Inside, a throng of conventioneering astronomers acknowledged Dr. Nystrom's distinguished presence with friendly quips and jesting catcalls.

Dr. Nystrom dismissed them with a wave of his hand and a mischievous smile.

"They won't be so jolly after this first meal," he said, chuckling lightly, to Ross and Dr. Ahn as they sat at a corner table. "Those jokers don't realize they're going to be eating recycled food. Take it easy, Ross, it won't make you sick, but you have to be, well, careful when you order."

"I don't like the sound of all this," Ross said uneasily. "Why can't I have real food, anyway?"

"Shipping costs are too steep," replied Dr. Nystrom. "But hold on a minute! Our organic chemists have protein synthesis almost down pat—"

"Almost?" said Ross, dubious.

"The only items on the menu that don't succeed are complicated dishes like steaks and fish. Stick with the simple fare; the cheese omelet is excellent. That's what I'm ordering and I commend it to you. Now if my guess is correct, those ground-bound types at the next table will have roast beef and salmon!"

Ross went along with Dr. Nystrom's suggestion. His omelet arrived promptly, and with enormous hesitation he tried a bite. Surprisingly, it tasted real. Better than real, in fact, especially when the other table was served with the more exotic synthetic fare. Soon Ross heard a chorus of dismayed groans as Dr. Nystrom's prediction was confirmed. Ross cleaned his plate.

"Please, have another," suggested a friendly voice. "It is served often on *Boreas*."

Ross glanced up, hardly surprised to see the pudgy director of operations hovering by his elbow.

"Subtlety is not Mr. Gurvich's strong suit," Dr.

Nystrom said to Ross, then he turned to the stout Russian and admonished "Dimitri! Mr. Moran has not accepted the job—or refused it. He is my luncheon guest."

"I see." Gurvich made an elaborate apology regretting his presumption, and backed away.

"I didn't know that you were aware of my situation, Dr. Nystrom."

"It's common knowledge on *Boreas* that we're shopping for a new meteorologist; when you showed up at the meeting with Tim I assumed you were it. Rather you were considering it. Otherwise you would have spoken about the job sooner."

There was a moment of silence around the table. Ross felt Dr. Nystrom's eyes on him, appraising him. He wondered what the judgment might be. Ross hoped it was favorable, for he was beginning to like Dr. Nystrom, and at last he admitted he was stumped.

"I don't know if I should take the offer or not," he said glumly. "I don't even want to think about returning home, but this whole deal's been weird from start to finish," he added, and then explained his forced flight from Los Angeles.

Dr. Nystrom lit his briar pipe. "Sounds like some top level strings have been pulled in your case for sure," he said finally. "But that's hardly rare. More than the U.S. Weather Service is interested in space, you know. There's the International Space Administration, first and most obviously, which is jointly run by the Soviet and American governments under a UN charter; then follow all the special interests: the communications industries and the various aerospace firms, too."

"And my employers," said Dr. Ahn quietly.

"That's right. The military. They're not supposed to be allowed in space at all, according to the Vienna treaty, but you can see a two-star general over at the table next to the bar," said Dr. Nystrom, pointing with his pipestem. "Don't stare too long, Ross, it gets them antsy. Actually, the treaty forbids only military hardware in space; the brass is free to roam about. I'd be hard put to say which group was tugging on your particular string . . . but certainly one bunch did!"

The words failed to penetrate. Inside Ross's head a voice was demanding *decide! decide! decide!* with an insistent rhythm, as though someone was banging a kettledrum in his ear. Quite suddenly the drumming halted and Ross straightened up, seeing his way clear at last. He knew what he wanted.

He wanted not to go back.

"I'm taking the job," Ross said firmly. The feeling of commitment was good. Whatever lingering doubts he held were swept away by Dr. Nystrom's enthusiastic reply.

"Wonderful! I was sure you wouldn't turn down old *Boreas* station for some ground-bound stint. Now if only my esteemed colleagues could make up their minds with equal dispatch—what wonders we'd see!"

Dr. Nystrom called for a telephone, and soon Ross informed the director of his decision. Gurvich replied with obvious relief that the remaining details, signing of contracts and related paperwork, could be handled by the administrative staff of *Boreas* itself. Ross was so distracted by the bureaucratic minutia that he failed to notice the two newcomers to the table until Gurvich wished him well and terminated the call circuit.

Tim was standing there, a girl at his side looking relaxed and happy. With the faintest tingling shock of recognition Ross saw she had been on the shuttle with him.

Her name was Christine Reney, Ross learned shortly. She had switched from the turquoise outfit to the traditional all-white uniform of her profession—complete to the little golden caduceus pinned to her collar. In all she seemed slim and incredibly beautiful standing there chatting with Tim, and Ross couldn't help but feel a slight needle of envy at his very singular good fortune.

Then their table phone rang. Dr. Nystrom picked up the receiver. His face darkened, and Ross thought he

40

banged down the receiver quite hard when he was through listening.

"That was flight operations," Dr. Nystrom announced. "The three of us," he said, looking at Ross and Tim, "are scheduled to leave for *Boreas* immediately, it seems."

"That's impossible!" Tim said. "I've got a four-day leave. This is only the second day."

"So did I," Dr. Nystrom said regretfully. "But just the same, the order stands. We'd better get walking."

"Whose order?" demanded Tim. "Eva's?"

"That's it exactly."

The little party started to break up. Dr. Ahn bowed slightly from the waist and excused himself. Christy walked with Tim and Ross and Dr. Nystrom from the cafe to the central elevator system. Tim kept a tight hold of Christy's hand until the door began to slide across the front of the elevator. Unwillingly he let go, watching with sad affection. Then the door shut and the car began rising.

At long last it deposited them in a carpeted waiting area faced with glass that overlooked the weightless hub of the station.

Directly before them hung a strange vehicle, an old space shuttle that had been declared unfit for atmospheric reentry. Shorn of its wings and tail surfaces and fitted with additional vernier jets, it was reborn as an orbital supply tug which would ferry the three of them from Main Station to *Boreas* in four hours, Dr. Nystrom told Ross.

Tim and Ross boarded the midsection and strapped themselves into the last remaining pair of seats. The rest of the cabin had been converted into cargo storage.

"Where'd the good doctor go?" Ross said.

"He's up front, in the command section. He's going to pilot the ship out."

Ross frowned. "Aren't these things automated?"

Tim smiled for the first time since he and Christy had parted company at the elevator.

"It is, of course, but the computer can be switched off. Then the tug's under manual control. That's Dr. Nystrom's biggest thrill. He's exactly like an old time aviator and likes nothing better than to steer it around by himself. There's the ten-second warning light. Hold tight!"

CHAPTER FOUR

Once the tug's engines cut off Ross lowered his chair back flat and instantly fell into a shallow and dreamless sleep. Precisely three hours later he awoke to an unusual sight.

At first, as his eyes opened, he heard a soft, but regular *tap-tap-tap* in the cabin, very much like falling rain. Rain? he thought. No way.

It was not rain. It was Tim, typing steadily away on a portable machine that he had clamped to a swing-out table. Ross could see that Tim had strapped himself to his seat, since everything in the tug was weightless while it climbed in an immense unpowered curve toward *Boreas*.

About all that Ross could see of Tim was his shiny boots sticking out from the white cloud that completely enclosed him. For an instant Ross imagined that somehow Tim was surrounded by a swarm of enormous pale butterflies, that they were about to settle on him any second now, while he *tap-tap-tapped* away, completely oblivious.

Belatedly Ross realized that the "butterflies" were many sheets of paper that Tim had discarded, and in the zero gravity of the tug, they remained exactly where he had put them. Ross peered closely at one of the sheets drifting nearby, supposing that it was probably a letter or a medical essay destined for some obscure

43

journal, but it proved to be neither. Instead there were the characteristic short paragraphs and inverted commas that indicated Tim was writing dialogue. Ross looked closer, then started reading silently. Two characters— a detective and an old woman—were discussing a murder.

"Are you writing a *mystery?*" said Ross.

The typing stopped.

"You're up," Tim's voice said from within the little paper nimbus; it was more of a statement than a question. Presently there was movement in the cloud and it started to thin as Tim plucked the manuscript from the air, sheet by sheet.

"Ninety, ninety-one. Ah, ninety-two," said Tim, gathering his work into a fat bundle.

"Come on," prodded Ross.

Nodding, Tim replied, "Well, it's no big secret. Writing's sort of my second occupation; it fills in the empty time on Boreas and if one of these books ever does sell. . . . Anyway, it beats staring out the window for hours on end. Speaking of which, what *is* outside?"

The Earth—a magnificent white crescent—and the stars. Only one other object was clearly visible to Ross: a sparkling point of light in a polar orbit far below the tug.

"Nothing else could be that bright," Tim mused. "It must be the manned station they call the *Basketball.* If we had a good strong telescope aboard you'd be able to see it's a huge aluminum-skinned balloon that looks like an old patched-up basketball. The military uses it to reflect laser beams, I think. Something like that."

They watched the satellite swing southwards across the frozen steppes of Russia.

"Dr. Nystrom told me the Vienna treaty didn't allow military equipment in space," Ross said, remembering his luncheon discussion.

"Only armed equipment," Tim returned. He started packing up his typewriter.

"That's a fine distinction."

Tim opened his mouth to reply, but the warning

buzzer cut him off and both of them hurriedly snapped their restraining belts tight. Thrusters started firing in sequence.

The view out was changing; Earth was sliding away to be replaced by Ross's first glimpse of *Boreas*. It looked like a steel drum turning about an axle silently in the distance.

There's home, Ross thought, feeling elated and a little scared at the sight of the station.

The tug edged up to a docking collar, there was a slight clank like an automobile door closing, and then Dr. Nystrom was entering the main cabin for the first time during the flight.

"Easy now," he said as the hatch opened and the pressure equalized with a faint whistle. Ross clambered over the threshold into the station's utility core where pumps and conduits carrying the four absolute essentials for life-support were concentrated: electrical power, water, oxygen, and computer functions. Large crimson WARNING stencils were everywhere, and Ross waited nervously as Dr. Nystrom and then Tim, lugging his typewriter, emerged and led the way down a short length of ladder into the gravity section of *Boreas* station.

Ross landed lightly on his feet. The downward pull was very feeble, but far preferable, he decided, than none at all.

They stood in a narrow white hallway leading to a wider corridor where Ross could hear the welcome sound of people talking. A few moments later he was in the corridor, being introduced to the owners of those voices. There were too many to keep straight the first time around, but he recalled two distinctly, a husband and wife team of photo-interpreters named Joel and Myra Colbert. Among the others was the station's computer technician and several dapper ISA officials who had just completed an inspection tour of *Boreas* and were waiting for the tug to be refueled and checked out before they could return to Main Station.

Ross turned down Myra Colbert's invitation to a cup

of coffee. His slight rest on the tug had been only a panacea for his weariness; it revealed how close to exhaustion he really was. All he wanted to do was find his room, shower, and sleep for a century.

"You think *Boreas* is a hotel?" said Tim, skeptically shaking his head at Ross. "Well then, you've got to sign in, first off."

"I don't think I follow you."

"You ought to meet the station commander, Eva Keough," Tim said. "And get the paperwork out of the way."

Ross gave him a look which Tim brushed aside. "Take it from the ole veteran, Ross. There'll be problems if you don't. Protocol, you might call it."

Ross had another name for it, and he didn't like the implication, but since he was still eager and curious to see *Boreas* despite his drowsy eyes, he agreed.

The administrative section of *Boreas* was situated at the opposite end of the station, a single large office bracketed by a complex warren of storage bays and lockers, utility cabinets, bins, sleeping quarters, and continuous snakes of plumbing and air recirculation ducts interlocking with fantastic precision. Inside the office a man sat at a computer console, keying in rows of digits.

He pointedly ignored Ross and Tim.

"I wish to see Ms. Keough," Ross said at last, yawning.

Without glancing from his keyboard, the man replied brusquely that the commander was not receiving visitors.

"Come again later," he told them in a chilly voice.

Ross shrugged and turned, intending to do just that, but Tim motioned for him to wait and he walked up to the console so that the light from the ceiling lamps was blocked by his wide shoulders.

The man behind the console scowled. "I said *later*."

Tim did not move a muscle.

Finally the man looked up, a sour expression on his face. He looked like he was in his late thirties, Ross

46

thought, and in spite of the camouflage of an expensive suit he was noticeably flabby, his glaring eyes sunk deep in his round face. He shifted his gaze to Ross and inspected him with plain condescension. "Who's that?"

"Our new meteorologist, Ross Moran," Tim replied. "Don't you think someone should detail him on his work here?"

"Not now, Diehle. The commander is occupied."

"Well, what about you?" Tim countered.

"I am also occupied." He returned to the computer.

"Look here," Tim said, "somebody'd better. The ISA didn't fly him all the way here for 'rec.'"

The man thrust a stack of forms into Tim's hands. "Get him to sign these. I will call Hanks," he said curtly and pressed a pad on the intercom before going back to the computer without another word or gesture to either of them.

Tim was seething with anger. When he and Ross were out in the corridor again, he said, "That pompous little—"

"But who is he?" Ross said, cutting in quickly in an attempt to divert Tim's accumulated fury.

"The commander's assistant. Name's Julian Martino, but around *Boreas* he's got a few others, too!"

What Ross could not do a gaunt man wearing bright yellow plaid pants and a heavy wool sweater did with no effort at all. He called to Tim from the nearest corridor junction; instantly Tim's anger disappeared.

So this was Hanks. Jonathan Hanks.

"Glad to make your acquaintance," he said genially. "By the way, if nobody's told you yet, I'm the fellow you're replacing. Hope you stick with the job longer than I could."

"You quit?" Ross asked as his curiosity took control.

"Not likely," Hanks said. "Got fired yesterday." He glanced at his watch and groaned. "We'd better get a move on, Ross. I'll show you the works, an' then leave you in peace."

Claiming hunger, Tim excused himself while Hanks went with Ross a short distance down the hall, pausing before a round opening in the end wall of the station's gravity section. Fitted around the aperture was a length of tubing a yard in diameter. The opposite end of it, Ross could see, was capped by a circular hatch.

"Down there," said Hanks, pointing, "is the zero-g part of the station, the place where you, my friend, will be earnin' your paycheck. Now watch carefully—this is tricky the first time."

Bending, Hanks grabbed a handrail. In one lithe motion he had swung himself inside the connecting tube and was effortlessly sailing toward the door. Ross wasn't so agile, but he managed to haul himself bodily into the revolving passageway, scraping against a projecting handhold only once. Hanks, meanwhile, had already unsealed and opened the plug-like hatch, and soon both of them were freely floating into a tiny chamber that linked the meteorology lab and the module containing the radio astronomy area.

Embedded in the bulkhead directly across from the tube exit was a heavily barred and sealed entrance. "Best not go snooping in there," Hanks remarked.

"What's the matter?"

"It's the direct accessway to the station's nuclear reactor."

Hanks led Ross into the meteorology lab. "Here we are," he told Ross, "the weather room. Last stop on the tour."

Ross gazed slowly around in awe-struck admiration.

The room was nearly spherical, studded with highly advanced electronic instruments, and since the lab was a zero-g environment its curving walls were entirely covered with this lavish carpet of sophisticated machinery.

"Ahh, that's just the secondary stuff," Hanks said. He turned and pointed to another hatchway on the other side of the room.

Ross poked his head in.

"Better have a good look-see," Hanks urged. So Ross gave a slight shove and found himself in the center of a huge plexiglas blister that faced out of the station's

48

metal hull like the orb of a Titan's eye, and the resemblance did not stop there. Packed into this turret were almost a dozen long-range telescopes, motion picture cameras, and still cameras, and an elaborate infrared scanner.

The associated control system was incredibly responsive, and Ross delightedly tested the hydraulics for several minutes. It was only when he emerged from the turret that he felt the staggering weight of responsibility settling onto him.

"Pah! This gear won't stick you with any hangups," Hanks assured him. "I had nary a one. It's all first-rate."

Then—it wasn't incompetence that got Hanks fired, Ross said to himself, puzzled. Why, he wondered, was this man being let go? And why am I taking over?

Hanks swept his hand over the smoothly functioning ranks of dials and meters and lights. "Don't fret unnecessarily; the computer regulates the details. You needn't worry about these machines while you're workin', Ross."

"But there's something else, isn't there?" said Ross slowly.

Hanks nodded.

"You mean Julian Martino or Eva Keough, don't you?"

"Her especially. She dumped me out of this job."

Ross was surprised to hear not the slightest trace of bitterness in his voice. It remained steady when he spoke after pausing to take a deep breath.

"She would do it again."

"I don't have the kind of practical experience you do," Ross said. "But my college time's behind me—my degree—and I have a contract for this job, too."

"And do you imagine for a second that I didn't?"

Ross felt stunned. "Then there's no reason—"

"You're right," Hanks replied flatly. "Fact is, though, I'm hunting for a new job. That's why I'm passing you this info, Ross. It *could* happen to you. The turret isn't an ivory tower."

The door to the weather room slid back to reveal a familiar figure, dressed to perfection in his expensive suit.

"Are your bags packed and ready, Hanks?" said Julian Martino. "The tug is about to undock."

"Don't get vexed; I'm not staying," Hanks told Martino. To Ross he gave a quick encouraging smile and started for the passageway tube, avoiding Martino at the door.

Martino watched him pass. His face was a cold mask devoid of emotion until he heard the tube door slam shut. Then Ross saw him allow himself a tiny self-satisfied grin before he turned away, leaving Ross alone in the lab.

CHAPTER FIVE

Raging gray clouds began closing around him as he fought with the plane's controls . . . Typhoon winds whipped the sodden cumulus into a solid, impenetrable curtain of darkness . . . He thought for a second that it looked like a cliff hanging in the sky, and pulled the plane into a shallow turning climb away.

The old jet moaned and shuddered, trying to tear itself away from him . . . He could hear shouting as the nose lifted wildly, sending men and machines and tape reels and books cascading to the tail . . . Then, a column of warm tropical air sucked in at the base of the hurricane went roaring up the cloud wall, seizing the port wing with the grip of a giant.

An indicator lamp glowed red; one of the engines was dying . . . The turbine bearings were hot . . . It could not endure the strain of the banshee wind . . . And the wind had infinite strength.

Without hesitation, he flicked switches, reducing the load on the failing engine, letting the other two take the brunt.

It was a mistake.

Inside the cockpit he heard a faint groaning . . . The sound of tortured metal tugging at itself, reluctantly stretching like cold taffy . . . First pliable . . . Then snapping apart . . . Someone was shouting while the jet slid into the clouds, aimed for the only calm within a hundred miles.

The eye of the typhoon . . . There, he thought, there was sanctuary.

On two engines the plane clawed toward freedom.

The clouds thinned . . . The grayness turned lighter, to the color of pewter . . . And then to silver . . . Closer, now, he thought.

An endless rumbling came into his ears . . . In moments it rose to a shriek . . . The fuselage began splintering . . . Muddy light flooded into the cockpit, and he turned, staring.

The entire tail assembly was gone.

No one tended the computers, no one sat at the radio board, no one watched the radar scanner . . . All had vanished . . . Paper, carpeting, bits of metal went streaming out into the brightening air.

Now the clouds were left behind as the plane disintegrated . . . Hurled into the eye by the explosive decompression, it fell at last.

He saw a filmy patch of blue sky . . . The white Capricorn sun flashed on waves below him . . . He tumbled down the open shaft of air, then his head slammed into something horribly hard and sharp . . .

Ross came awake. He could taste the fear in him.

For the slightest instant, as he crossed the half-world between sleep and full consciousness, he thrashed about in panic before he recognized his new bunk in his new room and felt the sheets damp with sweat. On a nearby shelf a blue light told the hour.

6:54.

He lay back. It was morning on *Boreas* station, almost time for the new day's work to begin.

Waiting there, his thoughts returned to the dream. How vivid it had seemed, and he wondered again if it had actually been like that—the end coming swift, brutal, and inevitable.

The clock chimed seven, paused, and chimed once

more. He got up to silence it and shot upwards, almost to the ceiling. He fell slowly and softly to the deck.

Got to watch myself in this reduced gravity field, he thought.

Though he'd purposely set the alarm early and dressed quickly, he heard brisk voices of other early risers and smelled bacon and coffee in the air. In the galley Joel Colbert and Tim were deep in conversation over their breakfast plates; Ms. Colbert was concentrating on a newscast beamed from Earth. Ross piled some scrambled eggs on his plate and very gingerly filled a cup with coffee and sat down beside her.

"Morning, there," she said, reducing the volume of the program. "You might be gratified to learn you're the very first new arrival to successfully pour himself coffee on the first attempt; a newcomer always seems to overestimate the gravity and manages to spill his coffee all over the deck. Congratulations!"

Myra Colbert was a large, rather motherly individual, so any shyness Ross felt that morning was quickly dispelled. For a while they talked and watched the newscast. On the screen the announcer was forecasting a new Asian war as the continent had suffered another drought year. With their population still rising and food stocks dwindling, Chinese leaders were demanding that part of Australia be opened to emigration to relieve the pressure on the mainland. The UN was meeting in emergency session, the announcer reported gravely and moved to the next story.

"Whew!" Myra Colbert said. "I'm glad to be here—when the shooting starts nobody's going to bother with dinky old *Boreas,* I hope!" She stood and switched off the television.

This was, Ross was to learn later, a kind of ritual signal that the meteorologists' work shift was supposed to begin. The Colberts left for the photo-interpretation section while Ross headed for the weather room, feeling an excitement and confidence in himself he thought he had forgotten.

Once in the turret, Ross checked the positioning

53

servos and the telescope controls twice, before he felt he could begin the task at hand. When the final relays had been inspected, he opened a switch and reported in.

"Activate the monitor, Ross," Joel Colbert said. Some distance away in their office-laboratory, the Colberts started their patient scrutiny of their battery of closed circuit color television screens.

"That's fine," Myra said. "Ross, why don't you turn on your own monitor and let's take a ride."

Ross did so, at once a bright color image of Earth sprang into life before his eyes, a duplicate of the telescope view the Colberts were observing.

It was incredibly lovely.

The globe was cleanly bisected by the terminator. Half lay in the shadow of night while the other fairly blazed with aquamarine, swirls of ivory and spots of ochre. The sun-mirroring Atlantic stretched between the cloud banks of Europe and North America. All of Asia and the Pacific slept in darkness, but the world's ceaseless rotation soon would pivot them into the light and bring dusk and evening to the West.

Ross turned his attention from those outer edges of the terrestrial sphere to the vital center, the Arctic Ocean.

This frozen sea, he knew well, was the most important place on Earth—from the weatherman's point of view. Much of the world's land mass adjoined the north polar regions and the two major oceans flowed into it, affecting the condition of the weather over the entire world.

Orbiting high over the northern tip of the Earth, *Boreas* was now in an excellent position to witness the slightest variation in the air currents moving over the icecap. On Ross's command, probes and sensory machines would peer down into the pulsing heart of a newly spawned storm, report a minor fluctuation in the air temperature, or track a blizzard and predict where it might roam.

"My screen's on here," he reported. "Ready back there?"

They were. Linked by their television and intercom network, Ross and the Colberts were an electronic team, and together they scanned the arctic cloud cover with the cluster of telescopes in the turret. Ross had to scramble to keep up with their instructions at first. The skills he had learned at college had grown rusty since graduation day. On the second sweep of their target, he happily felt his proficiency returning.

Then Joel called sharply, "Hey! I called for a hold. Wake up!"

Chagrined, Ross brought the turret back around and glanced quickly at the screen. There, nearly invisible in a ruffled blanket of white cloud, he noticed a characteristic trough-shaped depression.

"That's it," said Myra. "That's much better. Were you daydreaming up there, Ross?"

"A little, I think. I was preoccupied getting the hang of the controls." Ross looked at the screen again. The trough was still there. "That a storm cell?" he wondered aloud.

"Possibly," Joel said.

Ross cut to a stronger telescope, and the trough leaped closer. Now it seemed as though the clouds were only a hundred miles distant; another adjustment brought them within sixty miles, then to twenty.

The dish-shaped trough filled the screen completely, and it had the distinctive features of a storm cell: thick sidewalls topped by a thin layer of moisture. It was a tiny low pressure zone, a seed of energy with the potential to expand into a full arctic storm or to dissipate in a few hours. It was difficult to predict which way it might go. Ross decided to add a haze filter.

Now there was no doubt that the trough was a cell. The sidewalls stood out clearly.

Ross activated a strip-film camera, the infrared scanner and a thermocouple. Within seconds they had the precise altitude moisture content and temperature profile of the budding storm. The data was fed into the Colbert's forecasting computer.

The storm was growing, imperceptibly at the moment,

55

but soon it would acquire size and velocity as it swung south along the eastern tip of Canada. In a week it would be fanning out into the Atlantic tossing freighters and tankers; even the submarine fleet would be feeling the turbulence in the deeps.

The storm would break apart when at last it collided with the warm Gulf winds and it would rain in the Carolinas for days.

The computer flashed *end of predict sequence.*

"Okay!" Joel said, sounding pleased. "Let's have hard copy on all that, Ross."

This meant Ross had to assemble the film strips, the still photos which were automatically taken with every change in focus or filter, and the infrared stills, and process them as rapidly as possible for transmission to Earth.

The exposed films were stored on a multi-track cassette the size of a paperback book. Ross removed it and went to the processing machine installed on one of the walls of the weather room. He switched it on, inserted the cassette, and moved back.

Nothing happened.

What the . . .? Ross slid back over to the processor and hit the start button again.

Nothing happened, the machine hummed faintly. Ross tried the start controls a third time. A red signal blinked. *Warm.*

He stiffened. Warm? Why, the processor couldn't be overheating, could it? He thought frantically, ready to call for help when he saw a calibrated dial regulating the unit's temperature. He reset the dial ten degrees cooler.

Again, nothing happened.

Ross yanked the cassette out, reinserted it once more, this time taking special care that all the contact points lined up. He depressed the start button.

Nothing.

Ross swore in frustration and reached for the cassette. A green indicator lit up on the board. *Processing.*

That's better, Ross thought. There was a continuous

loud hum while the film unwound and passed through the chemical sprays that changed the raw stock into useable negatives. The green light winked out and was instantly replaced by another.

Processing completed.

The cassette popped out, dry.

He clutched it in one hand, gave a shove with the other toward the door and the Colbert's office.

Joel and Myra were busily preparing their part of the preliminary report on the storm cell. Joel took the cassette and set it aside for the moment, drawing Ross's attention to a stack of color transparents and prints.

"Jonathan didn't get around to taking care of this little detail," Joel said, handing Ross one of the glossy prints. To one side was a sizeable irregular distortion.

"Dust on the lens?"

"That's what I was hoping," Joel said. "But it appears a good deal more serious. That spot is a micro-meteor impact crater, which means, of course, that the lens on this particular 'scope will have to be replaced before we can use it again."

Ross groaned inwardly. This was no "small detail"; it was a five-hour task to dismantle the forward end of the telescope, replace the scarred lens, reconstruct the mounting, and adjust and recalibrate his instruments. And that was in normal gravity. He didn't even want to think of the time required when the myriad small parts would be drifting free inside the turret.

Myra gave him a sympathetic look. "Don't worry. We'll stay off your back until you have that glass fixed. Thanks for processing the film," she added, picking up the cassette.

Returning to the weather room, Ross hunted for the set of metric tools he would require, then entered the turret and started to work unscrewing the web of metal brackets holding the nine lenses and mirrors in position. As each section came loose Ross was careful to seal it in a plastic sack.

By the time he reached the ninth bracket the turret resembled an aquarium full of jellyfish. He reached inside the frame and withdrew the scratched lens. A close examination of its surface proved Joel's guess. The lens was smooth except for a roughened pit the size of the nail on his little finger.

The intercom rang.

"All right, hold your horses," Ross muttered, allowing the lens to float free while he thumbed the call button. "Moran here," he said, and cocked his head toward the speaker grille.

For a moment there was a confusion of voices, but soon one emerged clearly from the babble. "Ross, this is Joel. Look, something's gone awry over in your department."

"What do you mean?"

"Do you recall the film cassette you gave me."

Ross did remember, his heart thudding faster.

"There's something wrong with it. I don't know what it is, and Myra can't identify it either."

The other end of the line went dead for a second before a new voice, strident and demanding, came on the circuit.

"I want to see you in my office right away, Moran," said Julian Martino. "Drop what you're doing and get cracking."

An icy silence descended, then Martino spoke again.

"You had better get your explanations straight. The commander has informed me she wants to talk with you," he said coldly. "Afterwards."

CHAPTER SIX

Julian Martino looked like he might explode.

"Sit down," he commanded, and there was real fury compressed into those two words. They came rumbling out like thunder as Ross entered the assistant's office.

Martino went around behind his desk, opened a drawer, and extracted a small object. "Do you recognize this?" he said in a heavy tone.

"It's the film cassette I gave Joel Colbert," Ross replied, wondering what Martino was leading up to.

"That is—very good," said Martino with the slightest cutting edge of sarcasm. He doused the overhead lights. Ross heard a projector start to whirr and an instant later a wallscreen displayed one of the strip-films of Earth he'd taken. The shot was fuzzy and the colors seemed somehow wrong. Obviously the projector needed focusing, and Ross glanced nervously from the photo to Martino's shadowy bulk waiting for him to adjust the machine.

Martino returned the glance, his eyes dulled with a barely disguised animosity.

"I know what you're thinking; but the projector has been focused correctly beforehand. Maybe you wish to see another picture?"

He tapped a control and the cassette advanced.

The next image was a complete enigma, splotches of color strewn at random and maddeningly indistinct, as though grease was smeared on the negative.

The room lights came up, revealing Martino holding the film. With a contemptuous gesture he hurled it into a waste paper bin. "Useless junk. Hundreds of dollars and hours of valuable labor have gone for nothing. For nothing at all. Because you couldn't process a reel of film on an automatic device anyone on this station could operate perfectly well."

Ross swallowed with difficulty. There was a hollow sensation in the pit of his stomach that wouldn't go away.

"That processor was working flawlessly. It never gave anyone trouble. Except—someone reduced its internal temperature by ten degrees centigrade. I don't suppose you'd have any idea who would go and do such a thing?"

"I did it. The processor was overheating and I—"

"Correction, Mr. Moran, but it was not. And even if it was overheating, you wouldn't have known because you didn't even wait for it to warm up."

Ross closed his eyes. Warm. So that was what the machine was trying to tell him. It was so simple, the processor had to warm up before it would begin developing and washing the film. Why hadn't he seen that?

"So the film never developed completely and was ruined," said Ross, nodding to himself in disbelief.

Martino looked down at him. "I am not interested in any excuses you may offer. At this point I don't care. My one concern—my *only* concern—is making sure Earth receives the weather data from this station on schedule. This is a combined effort, nobody goes it alone.

"Am I making myself sufficiently clear? The next time you are tempted to alter conditions on your own whim or hunch, I assure you you will regret it. You may leave now, but remember that the commander expects

60

to see you in one hour. That's sixty minutes, Mr. Moran."

Ross was brooding over a stone-cold cup of coffee, thoughts running around and around in a dark, despairing circle. He hardly noticed—or for that matter cared—that another person had seated himself across the galley table from him.

"It can't be *that* bad," Tim said.

"Probably isn't," Ross admitted grudgingly. "Worst part is I deserved it. I really fouled up, and it was only right that Martino raked me over the coals."

"I was passing by and heard him yelling." Tim whistled. "There's no excuse for that kind of carrying-on."

Ross sipped the coffee and pushed it aside in disgust. "I expected to catch it, but Martino never gave me a chance to explain myself—or even apologize. He ran over me like a steamroller."

"That's his style, all right," Tim said with a nod. "He's trying really hard for the rep of a hot administrator. You know, the man who gets things accomplished. Regardless. That way he gets his name in circulation."

"What's he after?"

"Ten to one he's bucking for promotion to full commander," said Tim. Ross imagined he detected an old antagonism creeping into the young MD's voice, and guessed that the animosity ran deep into the past.

"Martino as ISA commander?" Ross said, wincing at the thought.

"Sure. He wants Eva Keough's command authority; now he's not much more than her hatchet man."

Ross smiled grimly. "He's not so bad."

"Only when he has everything in his favor. Otherwise, all he can do is bellow the way he did at you, and hope you'll stampede."

"Wait a minute!" Ross said. "I messed up, remember? Not Martino."

"Don't be so quick to defend the man," Tim replied.

"What do you mean by that?" Ross said sharply.

"Well, Joel Colbert was pretty upset about the whole incident. I had to give him a tranquilizer to get him settled down, and he told me those films weren't as crucial as Martino wanted you to believe. He said that he and Myra had already filed the report. The cassette was only backup material, and Joel was terribly rattled when Martino decided to raise such a stink over a non-essential item."

"Then why the steamroller act? Was he trying to get me mad at him?"

Tim shrugged. "On the evidence anyone would have to answer that one yes."

"But you don't, do you? Come on, master detective," Ross said, prodding. "Tell the jury."

Tim started laughing. "Hey, I only write them."

"You're dodging the issue."

"All right. Since you're so persistent, I'll tell you. But you won't like it."

"Go on."

All traces of his joking had vanished. Tim said, "I think he tried to set you up by intimidating you—forcing you into a corner you couldn't get out of, except on his terms."

"You're right. I don't like it, especially since I have to see Commander Keough soon," Ross said. Then, suddenly, he brightened. "If she hands me any of Martino's line, I've the best comeback in the world—the truth!"

"Just don't get overconfident," Tim said a little worriedly. "She's got plenty of influence, and you could get the axe the same as Hanks did. But don't get jumpy either. Maybe you'll find out what makes Eva Keough tick. Most everybody thinks she's naturally plain unpleasant."

The implication was obvious.

"And I take it that you don't?"

"Not at all," Tim said quietly.

Angular. That was the way Ross first saw Eva Keough's face, the bones beneath it making the shape

62

more angular than oval, stretching the skin into flat planes and lines devoid of even the slightest traces of fat or puffiness common in women of her age. At fifty-two, Commander Eva Keough was a striking woman. Once, Ross could see, she had been quite beautiful and some of that quality lingered on in her features, but now it was virtually submerged beneath the willful expression she assumed the moment he closed her office door.

Ross kept Tim's advice in mind, forcing himself to remain calm and refraining to speak first. It was effort wasted, though, for the commander was hardly as severe as tightly cropped silver-white hair and her immaculate ISA uniform at first suggested. She tactfully said nothing about the film, but directed Ross to a chair by her desk before she spoke.

"Mr. Gurvich was kind enough to transmit to me a copy of your college record," she began coolly. "I was impressed by your academic qualifications, and have readily agreed to your placement aboard this station."

"Thank you," Ross said in as noncommittal a voice as he could manage.

"You are aware, surely, that the ISA is granting you a substantial salary in exchange for your skills as a specialist in meteorology. No doubt you would be hard pressed to obtain a comparable post if you were returned to Earth."

Alarmed, Ross nodded.

"Oh, there is no cause for concern," she said in a cordial manner. "I am certain you and I understand one another. That is important; your predecessor, Mr. Jonathan Hanks, seemed to be unable to come to an understanding. He was insensitive to other crewmember's wishes, causing needless friction. He was warned repeatedly, but—" She allowed her voice to trail off.

Ross frowned. That didn't sound like Hanks.

The commander saw his reaction and replied, "Perhaps he gave you another reason, some rationalization, for his dismissal. It matters little, so long as you can avoid his type of behavior."

Vaguely Ross agreed, his thoughts elsewhere. He was thinking, she's holding back something from me, something important. But he couldn't imagine what.

"I spoke of friction," she continued. "By now you will have noticed that, despite my efforts, there is dissension aboard—quite mild—but dissension still the same. The station crew is no longer united, but has degenerated into self-exclusive cliques."

"My work keeps me pretty busy," Ross said, evading her gaze.

"Of course. You're new here and what I am discussing probably means little to you."

"I can see it's important," Ross said, hoping to draw her out. "I meant I haven't had the time to get to know everyone, and listen to what they say."

"Please understand I do not oppose the honest voicing of opinions. What I cannot abide is when it endangers the total efficiency of the station; then, regretfully I must take action."

She paused, looked at Ross directly, then went on.

"I thoroughly dislike doing so, but you can see that I am handicapped by my rank in these instances. People in charge always are the last to know when trouble is coming. What I need is some means to detect problems for me, before they disrupt the routine of productive work."

In other words, Ross thought, you want a spy. An informer.

"I have a complex assignment that leaves me little time or opportunity to concentrate on this very problem," she said, her voice softening, revealing a warmth that was missing before. Was she leading up to a personal appeal? he wondered. The final pitch after all this elaborate setting up? It was a chilling thought.

"I have need," she said, "of a person I can trust in these matters. Someone like you. You possess a fine intelligent and independent mind, and you can see the dangers these cliques pose to the station—to your work. But a few hours each week, simply to check and report, would be all I would require."

Ross felt his spine turn to ice. This was the most outrageous invitation he'd ever gotten, and he barely kept his temper from exploding.

"I don't think so."

"Excuse me," Eva Keough said, starting. "I don't believe I understand you."

"Oh, I believe that you do."

Her eyes narrowed to suspicious slits. "Who has been talking to you?"

Ross said nothing.

"Who was it?" she demanded, furious. "Was it Diehle? Nystrom?"

"Guess I'm just not interested in your offer," Ross said, marveling at his self-control. "Like you said, I'm new around here. My work keeps me pretty busy."

"You are making a serious error, Moran," she said, but the words were hollow and empty. The battle, such as it was, now was finished. She had lost, and she probably wanted to shout at him. Instead, she remained perfectly still.

And that's not much of an accomplishment, Ross thought as he walked out. After all *her* job is keeping things in control.

But the sheer gall! Ross shook his head, almost in amusement. Thinking she could snap her fingers and flash!—there was Ross Moran, confidante and secret agent for Commander Eva Keough.

It was so absurd he laughed. Then his laughter faded, and he wondered how many others she had similarly approached, and how many succumbed? Why, she might have one or more of her own people planted in the station staff already, listening.

Better watch my step, he told himself. And my tongue. He glanced around. The hallway was silent. All clear.

Right there he caught himself. Damn! I'm turning paranoid. I'm letting myself scare myself, he thought. He broke the chain of thought and started back to the turret.

With wrench and screwdriver in hand again, Ross

grappled with the unwieldy telescope frame, fitting the brackets into their places. He ripped open the ridge of his knuckles on a protruding screw and ignored the stinging for as long as he could. Finally it grew raw and painful. Ross wormed his way out of the turret and went searching for a first-aid kit.

There was supposed to be a kit attached to the wall in the connecting corridor, right beside the pressurized fire extinguisher and fireaxe. There was no sign of the kit there.

A thin stream of blood was flowing from the cut, hovering like a wet crimson thread. The medical dispensary was at the other end of *Boreas,* Ross thought, and this cut isn't worth the trouble to go there. Perhaps Dr. Nystrom had the kit, he said to himself. Wasn't that his voice, issuing faintly from the radio astronomy module?

The lab door was partly open. For a moment Ross heard the drowsy hum of electrical equipment. He must be in, Ross thought, allowing himself to drift forward with his other hand clamped over the cut.

Something was going *thump* occasionally beyond that door.

Ross called out for Dr. Nystrom. There was no reply.

Thump! The door vibrated under a slight impact. That did it. Ross pushed it open, unsure of just what he would encounter.

It wouldn't be Dr. Nystrom. That was plain enough after a single glance showed him absent from his little domain.

Then something shot by with incredible speed, looping in midair spectacularly before it headed back toward Ross. He yanked himself from its path, watching it circle the lab. It darted at him again, wings all ablur, then halted and hovered effortlessly like an iridescent emerald bullet.

The bullet peered at Ross with tiny eyes, like drops of water. Ross stared back at the hummingbird in complete astonishment. It continued to regard him for a few seconds, then it folded its wings back along its sleek creamy white flanks, making no protest when Ross gently enclosed it in his hand.

Several inches overhead was a large cage with its wire gate hanging open, enabling Ross to restore the situation to normal without waking the sleeping creature.

Still no first-aid kit, Ross thought, after all that. He nursed his wound and wondered where Dr. Nystrom had stowed it. He checked the obvious places first and discovered it, at long last, floating behind the open door. He took a spool of bandage with him and was closing the lab door behing him when he came face to face with Timothy Diehle.

Ross greeted him with flustered surprise, adding, "I thought you were in the dispensary."

"And I thought *you* were talking with the commander," Tim said. "Dr. Nystrom in?"

"Why, no. I thought so too, but he's not."

"What's the matter with you, Ross? You're awfully jumpy. Eva give you a hard time?"

"Not really," Ross replied. He gave Tim a quick sketch of their conversation, but decided to omit her request that he turn snoop for her. That's one item best left unrepeated, he thought, and one forgotten as soon as possible.

"That's her, all right," Tim said when Ross finished. "She never loses her cool."

Ross had to grimace. "Martino fills in for her there."

"True, true. They're quite a team when you stop to think of it. Like an old time vaudeville act: the howler monkey and the wise old owl. It'd be funny if they weren't so serious and methodical, trying the same approach on everyone they tried on you. You'd think they'd loosen up, wouldn't you? Well, let me know when Dr. Nystrom returns, OK?"

Ross agreed. After bandaging his hand he went back to the still dismantled telescope. He was adjusting the azimuth controls when one of Tim's phrases hit him like a shock: *trying the same approach on everyone they tried on you.*

Everyone.

How could that be true? That meant Eva Keough and Julian Martino had—sometime—approached Tim. And it followed they probably asked him to do their spying. Ross wondered which of the crew they might have wanted Tim to observe. Dr. Nystrom?

No. And yet, the commander had spoken *that* name with unmistakable vehemence, he did recall. Then he remembered Tim's name had been included, also. Obviously he hadn't gone along with the suggestion. But the fact remained, probably he had been asked to spy on his friends. The seeds of suspicion had been planted.

The breath seemed to whistle out of him.

Tim had seen him coming from Dr. Nystrom's lab right after the commander had talked with him. Could Tim be thinking that he had become an informer for her? That he'd been searching in Dr. Nystrom's personal efforts, hunting for scraps of incriminating evidence?

There was no way of knowing, he reasoned. But reason took nothing away from the most obvious conclusion.

From circumstantial events, Tim had every justification to believe Ross had become a turncoat. Every single one.

CHAPTER SEVEN

Clearly, something was bothering Dr. Alfred Nystrom.
"He's become a recluse, almost," Ross said.

It was a week later, when Ross felt he had recovered
Tim's confidence sufficiently to talk over matters of
mutual concern. They were sitting at a table in the
galley.

"Sure, I've noticed it," said Tim. "He's always in his
lab working, I guess—anyway the door's shut all the
time. But I don't think it indicates anything in particular."

"He's completely different from the way he was on
Main Station," Ross countered. "You never see him,
and when you do he looks worried about *something*."

"That just means he's hard at work when he holes
up in the radio astronomy lab like this. I will admit he's
onto something important, since he's been putting in
eighteen hours a day on it so far!"

Tim would have continued, had not the object of
his previous sentence walked into the room.

"So you two are here," Dr. Nystrom exclaimed. "The
whole crew's been looking for you, though why they
never poked their heads in here I'll never know."

"So where else can you have coffee and idle conversation this early in the day? Anyhow, why all the rush?"

"Eva has called a meeting in the lounge. The crew has assembled there already, except for you two, and they're waiting."

As if on cue the galley lights went dead and were replaced by the watery blue glow of the auxiliaries, casting deep shadows around them. It was the same whichever way they went in the branching corridors, even in the lounge itself.

The station staff was standing or sitting at a group of tables, presided over by the commander and her assistant, who had his arms folded confidently across his chest.

Ross, Tim, and Dr. Nystrom found chairs in the rear of the room, and Eva Keough began to address them.

"I have called you from your regular duties because something has occurred that concerns all of us aboard this station. It is operating now on secondary power supplies, the storage batteries and fuel cells, as I have ordered the nuclear reactor shut down indefinitely. The reason is this, a plutonium slug, one of the essential power elements, has seriously deteriorated, making the reactor hazardous to keep in operation. I have obtained permission to suspend all work until the rod is replaced."

There was a murmur of voices in the eerily half-lighted lounge.

"This does not mean a vacation," Commander Keough told them flatly. "Quite the opposite. Were these ordinary circumstances a repair team would be brought from Main Station to perform the task. This would require three days, too long to delay, and so I have decided to replace the faulty element with another from the station's stores.

"The supply tug will be used as the base of operations and will be headed by my assistant, Julian Martino. He and the station's electronics specialist, Alan

70

Essenfield, have been briefed on the procedure, and Dr. Nystrom will be assisting them. Ross Moran will remain aboard the tug and keep watch."

"Didn't know you volunteered for this," whispered Tim.

"Me either," Ross said, coming out of his daze.

Shortly, Ross was boarding the tug.

He received a fast run-through from Martino on his part in the operation, which primarily consisted of keeping track of the progress and relaying messages back to the station, while the other three went outside in their suits. Secretly Ross was hoping to be allowed to suit up and accompany them, but Martino quashed that immediately.

"You stay put in the ship's nose and keep your eyes open. Don't let any one of us get out of your sight at any time."

Soon the tug was in position, having been edged around the perimeter of *Boreas* until the reactor came into view at the tip of its two-hundred foot long boom which extended from the nonrotating end of the station. Dr. Nystrom parked the little craft a safe distance from the massive chunk of steel. Ross helped him and Julian Martino into their white spacesuits. Alan Essenfield, a soft-spoken, gangling fellow, slipped into his with practiced dexterity and led the repair crew to the cargo airlock, pausing only to pick up the fresh plutonium fuel slug packed in a lead cylinder.

The lock cycled and the three of them stepped out into space.

Ross hurried forward to the cockpit, a bubble of toughened plastic. He set up the communications linkages between the men outside and the receiver aboard *Boreas* and rotated the ship slightly to provide the widest possible view of the reactor.

"We're ready," said Dr. Nystrom's voice, crackling in the speaker. He didn't sound full of confidence, Ross thought.

The three figures were stationary before the reactor now, the new bar of plutonium was tethered a way off, and the repair team was studiously avoiding it: a sensible precaution, since not only was it intensely radioactive but it had a furiously hot temperature of 430 degrees centigrade inside its protective casing.

"Essenfield and Martino are opening the outer ring seals," Dr. Nystrom reported a minute later.

They waited while Dr. Nystrom handed Martino a casing to hold the deteriorated power slug still inside the reactor. When both the outer and inner seals were opened, Alan Essenfield would extract the spent slug with a special tool and slide it into the tube Martino held. Then they would reverse the procedure with the new plutonium bar, finally sealing up the receptacle and returning to the tug. Just like changing fuses, Ross thought, watching the white-clad figures huddle around the reactor.

"The outer seal is open," said Dr. Nystrom. "Now he is unlocking the inner one and—"

Alan Essenfield was caught full in the chest by an enormous burst of highly compressed gas. It threw him a dozen feet aside, his arms flailing. Almost instantly the geyser thinned to nothingness, but there was still pressure enough remaining in the receptacle to ram the plutonium slug out of the reactor like an angry black barracuda.

Dr. Nystrom shouted a warning as the slug shot out.

Julian Martino probably never heard the cry. He was preoccupied with prying the cap from the casing in his hand, his left arm raised over the faceplate of his helmet as he wrestled with the tightly closed lid with all his concentration. It was the only thing that saved his life.

Thrust free of the reactor the slug smashed into his forearm and elbow and charred the suit fabric into a dark smear. In the collision the slug lost its kinetic energy, passing it along to Martino who went cartwheeling in reaction. As the assistant tumbled by, Dr. Nystrom grasped his arm and called out for Alan Essenfield to help.

Ross saw it all.

He stared in horror for a second, then brought his hand down on the single red-rimmed key on the communication panel. It radioed to the computer screen on *Boreas* the notation:

EMERGENCY

EMERGENCY

EMERGENCY

and simultaneously the tug quivered as twin flares outlined the three men with a brilliant blue-white light.

Dr. Nystrom steadied Martino's thrashing body and pulled him to the open airlock. Ross heard it cycle, and then the hatches slid back.

"Help me get his suit off," Dr. Nystrom commanded.

Ross sprang forward and tugged at the fastening strip on the side of the suit. He found the complete lack of gravity made every motion difficult and reached for a better hold.

"Ross!" shouted Dr. Nystrom, "don't touch that arm, it's seething with radiation."

Martino stopped struggling and lapsed into unconsciousness. Dr. Nystrom removed Martino's helmet and at last the fastening split apart. While Dr. Nystrom went forward to start up the tug's engines, Ross wriggled the suit off Martino, and then gathering the bulky material in a bundle he stowed it in a bulkhead compartment.

"Wait! What about Essenfield?" Ross said.

"We'll get him later," replied Dr. Nystrom. His fingers touched the vernier controls and Ross could feel a burst of acceleration. They drifted for a few moments, then Dr. Nystrom guided the ship into the docking collar and let open the cargo hatch. Ross scooped up Martino and lifted him into the station.

Tim gasped at the sight of the burnt and bloody arm.

"Come on, we'll both carry him to the dispensary," he said. When they arrived with the limp body Tim started to work quickly, but with great care, and soon Martino's pulse responded.

Then it began to fall. Desperately, Tim clipped an oxygen mask over the wounded man's face and injected a vial of some clear drug directly into the vein of the left arm, just above the elbow. He disposed of the syringe and stood up, shaking.

"That should hold him," he said, feeling the pulse count rise.

Nobody had noticed Commander Eva Keough entering the dispensary until she spoke.

"Good," she said impassively. "Stay with him."

Tim nodded. "Of course. He should be moved to the Main Station hospital. They have facilities for adequately treating radiation burns."

"No," said Eva Keough.

"What? He can't stay here," said Tim, urgency in his voice.

"I say he remains aboard this station. He will not be removed without my consent."

"But, Commander—"

"I think your patient is coming round," she said firmly.

Ross had expected Tim to explode with rage. However, the doctor diverted his attention to Martino, whose eyes now were beginning to flutter open. He groaned in pain, and Tim administered another injection, then set to cleaning the burn with a plastic-foam sprayer. The foam bubbled up, carrying to the surface the burnt tissue and the remaining particles of charred fabric where they could be skimmed off and the foam removed. The burn was clean and Tim was bandaging it when Ross decided to return to the lounge. Ross heard Dr. Nystrom's voice, hoarse and anxious, as he walked in.

". . . but the man's been hurt badly," Dr. Nystrom protested.

"I realize that, and I appreciate your offer to transport him to Main Station," said the commander. "But I have decided he will remain here for the present."

74

"That's a severe injury, Commander. Please reconsider."

She turned and looked at Dr. Nystrom, undisturbed that several crewmembers were watching.

"I have complete confidence in our physician's competence to treat the wound. Could it be, Dr. Nystrom, that you do not share this confidence?"

Dr. Nystrom snorted. "That's utter nonsense."

"Come now, be honest. Don't you really doubt the abilities of every person on this station, yourself excluded?"

Now that was nonsense, Ross thought, seeing Dr. Nystrom redden involuntarily.

Eva Keough added, "You are annoyed, I think, not because a fellow staff member has been injured, but because your own professional duties have been interrupted. No? Tell me then, why else were you so reluctant to join the repair squad? Was that nova you have found so important?"

"Not at all, but since you've decided to broach the subject anyway, don't you think it is strange that the one time I have come to you with a request not to be disturbed—a time when I really need my lab equipment in constant use—you decide to cut the power off? And being in such a rush that you can't possibly wait for some professional nuclear engineers, you send four amateurs out to do the job. One gets hurt and—"

"This is neither the place nor the time to discuss this matter, I think. If you should decide to pursue it, let me remind you that under the ISA charter you could be held for insubordination. I suggest you consider that fact, Dr. Nystrom."

And she turned and stalked out of the lounge.

Dr. Nystrom sat on a hassock and stared glumly off into a corner. His shoulders sagged.

"She wouldn't actually try to back up that threat," Ross asked. "Would she?"

"Oh, it's not likely," replied Dr. Nystrom. "After all, a trial would bring up her role in this mess, too. I really don't imagine she wants *that* kind of publicity. But there's one detail both of us overlooked completely.

"We were supposed to return in the tug and get Essenfield. Remember?"

Ross nodded. "He elected to stay outside. Is he all right?"

"Fine. In the commotion I forgot he was still suited up and near the reactor. In a way it doesn't really matter. Alan's an old spacehand, and he jetted back to the air lock about five minutes ago."

Ross calculated quickly. "Then he was outside for fifty-five minutes, alone."

"He didn't just bide his time," said Dr. Nystrom. "He corralled the escaped fuel slug in its casing. And then he also accomplished what all four of us were supposed to do in the first place."

"You mean he set in the new fuel element too? By himself?"

"Didn't you notice that the main lighting was turned on again?" said Dr. Nystrom, with a faint smile.

It was true. The dim blue bulbs and the deep black shadows that had once filled the lounge were gone, and the room was cheerfully lighted by the ceiling fluorescents. Ross saw, as if for the first time, that the paintings on the walls glowed with oil colors.

Dr. Nystrom was digging through his pockets for pipe and tobacco. Once the mixture was lit, he continued.

"Don't you grasp what this means? Eva Keough, it turns out, was completely correct in her judgment, a team of engineers wasn't needed to refuel the reactor.

"Alan did the work perfectly well, all by himself. One man, alone. And I keep thinking to myself that maybe she was right about my work, also. Maybe that nova I've been observing did distract me out there."

"I don't believe it for a minute," Ross said. "And I was watching the three of you at the time it happened. You did everything possible."

"Thanks," replied Dr. Nystrom. "Maybe I'm simply

76

imagining things. But then, that nova's awfully important to me. If it took away even a bit of my attention, well, maybe Martino wouldn't be lying in the dispensary now with that terrible gash in his arm."

CHAPTER EIGHT

Ross was standing behind a low granite revetment overlooking the endless expanse of the sea. Waves splashed on a faraway beach. The sun rode the horizon like a crimson ship.

If he closed his eyes a little and let the scene blur, then the craggy coastline seemed real. Well, real enough to bloc out the fact that Ross was in the envirotape library on *Boreas*.

After a while the sounds of the sea faded. A phantom orchestra materialized on the worn stones and began playing a Mozart concerto. The mood was complete. Ross shut his eyes and tried to relax.

But it was easier to program a peaceful illusion than to forget the hard knot of tension that was plaguing him.

Several weeks had passed since the reactor incident. Eva Keough had quickly recognized the dangerous emotional condition of the station crew and instituted a less rigorous schedule. She also eased up on them, not a difficult task with Julian Martino still confined to his dispensary bed. For a while life seemed normal, even enjoyable at times like these.

Then, with infinite subtlety, the ugly emotion returned.

Fear.

Ross felt it himself now. He flinched at unexpected

noises, started when people addressed him suddenly or even when a friendly greeting caught him unawares.

He was expecting a blow that never came, and worse, he did not know why.

The warm tones of the French horns muted, to be replaced by steady footfalls from behind. They stopped abruptly.

"You look like a man enjoying himself," Tim said.

"More than you'll know," Ross said, relieved.

"I've used the simulator tapes myself, but not this particular scene. Never had an interest in old stony castles."

"Well, it's not so bad," Ross said. "Sit down and indulge your fantasies."

"That would be nice" Tim sounded distracted and distant, and Ross wondered if Martino was presenting problems. That was not the case.

"Then what *is* bugging you?" said Ross.

"Is it that obvious? It is? Well, you're right. It's an odd thing, something I wouldn't have brought up, except for your asking."

"Yes, yes, now stop stalling," Ross said, laughing.

"Well, it is serious. When I went to see Dr. Nystrom a while ago his door was open just a crack, but he wasn't around."

"That's hardly odd," Ross said, recalling his own experience that had started out exactly that way and wound up with a small bird.

"It was just outside, right near the door frame, when I smelled it."

"It? What are you driving at?" Ross began to suspect an elaborate prank.

"This peculiar smell. It was exactly like," Tim seemed to halt and search for the phrase, "like pine trees."

"That's all?"

"No, wait. First off I thought it was an aeromatic. A cleaning fluid or air freshener, perhaps. But then I remembered the ISA has banned strong-smelling substances on all space vehicles because the air recon-

79

ditioning equipment can't cope with those odors. The filtration screens are too delicate, I guess. The regulation is quite strict."

"I should hope so," replied Ross. "If the air system died, we'd all follow fairly quickly. How about a leaky can of illicit after shave lotion, then?"

Tim considered that. "Don't think Dr. Nystrom would take the chance of being caught with it. If Eva found it, he'd be expelled from *Boreas*. The ISA is strict about that rule! Even my medicinal sprays are especially neutralized to avoid trouble."

"If you're putting me on—" Ross said. "All right, let's go find out."

He switched off the tape and sea, sun, and castle vanished.

In a few minutes they halted outside the radio astronomy lab. "It was right here," Tim said earnestly.

Ross inhaled slowly.

"Nothing unusual," he told Tim and meant it. Ross had a sensitive nose.

"Well, it was here," Tim said firmly. "And it was *real,* the same as the spruce and pine forests in the Rockies I went camping in. It was real, I tell you!"

Ross suggested that the air cleaners might have dispersed the peculiar odor. And then he had another idea, and he persuaded Tim to return to the tape library with him. After selecting a taped scene, Ross dropped the reel into the playback.

The harsh white walls softened to a shadowy green. The darkness swelled around them as a wind seemed to arise from nowhere, and they were plunged into a forest glade.

"Do you smell the trees now?" Ross said as the ghostly woods swayed.

Entranced, Tim nodded. Then he shook his head in bewilderment. "I see what you're driving at now. That I'd been thinking of pine trees—and imagined I smelled them?"

"Something like that. Autosuggestion."

"Guess it was pretty foolish of me to bring it up,"

said Tim in a self-conscious whisper. "Sorry to bother you."

Ross sat thinking after Tim left. He didn't doubt his friend's story, bizarre as it was, and he felt curious enough to have another look around the corridor outside Dr. Nystrom's laboratory. Once more he found nothing to substantiate Tim's account. The place was empty, silent, and odorless.

Almost silent. Ross could hear the drone of electronics descending in pitch inside the radio astronomer's module, and he thought maybe the scientist could further the inquiry.

"Who's there?" came Dr. Nystrom's startled voice after Ross tapped on the door, but as soon as he identified himself Ross was let in. Dr. Nystrom said, "Please pardon my suspicion, but I thought you were somebody else come knocking. Anyway, I am glad to see you. There's something I want to show you."

Ross followed Dr. Nystrom through his fantastic little realm of oscilloscopes and amplifiers to a small device bolted to the wall. It turned out to be a zero-g percolator.

"Have some coffee while I clean Whit's quarters."

"Whit? That the name of your hummingbird?"

"Exactly, and since you two have already met I shall skip the introductions," said Dr. Nystrom, brandishing a cordless vacuumer like a pirate cutlass at the untidy birdcage. Whit viewed the proceedings with disdain, then swooped wildly about before darting obediently back into his cage.

"Always the showoff," said Dr. Nystrom admiringly. "Exactly like his namesake, Walt Whitman, though I do suppose that is the only trait they have in common."

"He doesn't resemble any poet I've ever heard of," Ross replied, gratefully accepting the warm bulb of coffee Dr. Nystrom set before him. The lab was chilly, the coffee hot, and for some time he forgot his original reason for going there.

"Tim wants to see you," Ross said, remembering at last.

Dr. Nystrom nodded. "He's been after me for weeks to take a physical. But I simply haven't had the opportunity since I began observing the nova in the constellation Auriga last month."

"He mentioned that."

"Did he tell you that now Oxford University has agreed to share their data on the nova with me? In fact, they persuaded the ISA to orbit a little relay satellite to pass along signals between us during the periods when *Boreas* orbits beyond direct contact with England. Radio astronomers all over the world are planning to help, too. Isn't it marvelous?"

He fairly bubbled over with enthusiasm, and continued for a while outlining the details of the joint project. For the most part, however, Ross found it difficult to understand Dr. Nystrom's fascination in a star exploding many light-years away. It was too remote from his own life and too removed from the affairs of Earth. What, he asked Dr. Nystrom, had it to do with, say, the threat of war between China and Australia?

"Very little, I will grant you, if you see it only that way," replied Dr. Nystrom after a minute. "But already today I learned that *Nova Aurigae* is affecting some people. Commander Keough has been trying to persuade me to have the relay satellite removed from orbit."

Ross frowned and asked, "Won't that mean the end of your experiment?"

"More or less. If the relay is deorbited I won't have the direct contact with the ground station this kind of observation requires."

"What's wrong with the relay satellite, then?"

"As far as I can tell, nothing. But she contends that its orbit will shift soon so that it intersects the path of the *Basketball* and so presents a danger to its crew."

"Sounds serious."

"It would be," replied Dr. Nystrom, "except space is vast and their respective orbits are hundreds of miles apart. The chance of a collision is infinitesimal."

Ross drained the last of the coffee from the bulb.

"Why don't you ask the International Space Administration to investigate her claims. As I recall the ISA is supposed to insure the safety of all space vehicles."

"A board of inquiry has already decided in my favor, but she's still trying to change my mind. Seems the matter can't wait. She wants the relay deorbited immediately."

"Hasn't she learned about trying to rush things from Martino's accident?" Ross said, amazed.

"That!" Dr. Nystrom's eyebrows climbed. "She claims the reason the plutonium was ejected was because the last time the reactor was flushed out with carbon dioxide not all the gas was drained off properly and enough remained to almost do in Julian Martino. My guess is she figures if the so-called experts aren't responsible for their own work, she'd better do it herself. Speaking figuratively, of course."

"Are you going to have the relay satellite removed?"

Dr. Nystrom replied by shaking his head vigorously. "Why should I have my work here interrupted needlessly another time on account of her fears. I'll let the ISA straighten this mess out."

Ross was impressed that Dr. Nystrom believed deeply enough in himself and his own work—and in *Nova Aurigae*—to risk the wrath of his superior. And later he wondered if he also possessed that kind of courage, for he was starting to realize that the time was approaching when he might be forced to find out.

CHAPTER NINE

The monster was growing. For five nights and six days they watched it forming out of random eddies of low and high pressure, until the storm was a thousand miles across. They watched as it drew strength from the wan winter sun and thrust a ferocious stormwind laden with biting ice crystals to sweep around its perimeters. They watched and photographed and measured and probed for almost a week before they knew what it would do next. By then it was clear. This monster, this terrible storm, had grown too huge and powerful to remain in the confines of the Arctic. It was turning south.

Ross touched the hydraulic control levers and the telescope slid back into its housing with an oily hiss. He extracted the exposed film cassette from the telescope and went to process it, but he found his thoughts returning to what he had been working on recently.

From his vantage point in the turret, the new storm on Earth was extraordinarily simple to locate, even though the region around the North Pole was completely shrouded in the long winter night. The storm was a faint gray patch hovering almost exactly over the center of the northern hemisphere. Ross could distinguish little else in the inky darkness, but it was an indication of how well the intensive schedule of observations on *Boreas* had sharpened his senses. A month earlier, his untrained eyes would never have been able to discern the storm's irregular outline from the details surrounding it.

He glanced up, the clock on the wall of the weather room read 12:01 A.M., December 31, 1995. The first minute of the last day of the year. In another twenty-four hours 1996 would come rolling in. But not here, Ross thought, and he smiled to himself.

A mammoth New Year's celebration was planned on Main Station, and he was going. Tim had wangled a couple of invitations weeks beforehand; now both he and Ross were looking forward to attending the party with something like longing. It would be their first leave from *Boreas* in two seemingly endless months. Tim was eager to see Christy again. Ross was eager to see anyone new.

Especially anyone who had never heard of, seen, or was interested in *Boreas* station. *Cabin fever,* Tim called it once. *The feeling of being cooped up in close quarters with only a few, a very few number of people around. After a while the routine and the isolation get to you.*

Cabin fever. Well, he thought, a long and leisurely stay on Main Station would banish that.

Right now the only obstacle standing in their way was the not inconsiderable problem of transportation. According to schedule the weekly run of the supply tug from Main Station to *Boreas* and return would not be for four more days. In four days the party would be nothing more than a memory, done and gone by the time they arrived. The obvious and simple solution was to change the schedule, but the only person with the authority to do so wasn't cooperating.

Ross dropped off the finished film at the Colberts' office and hurried over to the dispensary to ask Tim if Commander Keough had changed her mind. As he walked down the corridor, dimmed to simulate "night" on the station, Ross wondered if the dispensary would still be open.

He was lucky.

"The Doctor is in," Tim announced portentously. "You may enter."

Ross indicated Tim's desk clock and said, "You keep odd business hours, doc."

"So do you," Tim replied. "I've been running an inventory of supplies and I find I'm missing a carton of oxygen capsules. Help me look for it in the central storage bay?"

Ross followed the movement of Tim's eyes to a curtained-off area at the back of the dispensary where he was sure he could hear muffled breathing sounds emerging with heavy regularity. So that's it, he thought. At that, Tim looked visibly relieved, and then led the way down a level to a large room near the supply dock.

"Glad you picked up on that, Ross. The walls of *Boreas* may not have ears, but I'm certain my patient does."

"And you actually believe Julian Martino was listening in?"

Tim nodded seriously.

"Hey, come off it," Ross said lightly. "Cabin fever must be really getting to you if you start imagining that."

"I'm not turning paranoid," Tim said defensively. "I'm just not taking any chances anymore of being overheard."

"You know, you do look scared," said Ross, becoming concerned. For the first time he noticed Tim's normally ebullient features had changed. He now appeared drawn and tense.

"I am, in a way. Been like this since the last tug arrived with the mail from Main Station."

"That was last Thursday."

Tim nodded again.

"You remember Jonathan Hanks, don't you?" he continued. "Well, he got himself a new job on Main Station, repairing and servicing the computers in the hospital section. Medical histories, records of prescriptions and everything else is stored in the computer memory banks so the medical staff can quickly refer to them.

86

In an emergency operation, for instance, you have to have some sort of background on the patient immediately. Well, one time Hanks decided to have a peek, and so he programmed the computer to print out the files of Eva Keough and Julian Martino."

Ross frowned. "Isn't that slightly illegal? I mean, aren't those records supposed to be private?"

"Technically no. There's no law because only the hospital staff know the computer programming techniqe. But Hanks doped it out on his own. Enough of it, at least. Once he saw what he had uncovered he was too nervous to act on it. Instead, he wrote me a letter with all the gory details."

"Gallstones and appendectomies?"

Tim shot him a cold look. "Hardly. The files showed that both of them were officers in the military on Earth, in NATO, back in the late 1980s. And both of them resigned their commissions in order to join the ISA, because according to the ISA charter only civilians can be employed."

"That makes sense," Ross replied. "The treaty of Vienna banned military work in space, so now they're in line with the treaty, right? Then what's your problem?"

"Just this. Simply resigning a commission doesn't turn an officer into a civilian, Hanks found out. All it means is that the person isn't an officer any more. He's still tied to the service."

"Then both of them are violating the ISA charter and the treaty while they are aboard *Boreas*."

"And nobody seems to care," Tim added. "Well, I still have to find those capsules while I'm here."

Ross got to his feet and helped Tim search the room, starting at the front wall and working toward the rear bulkhead through a labyrinth of aisles between piles of supplies stacked almost to the ceiling. Sometimes Ross found his way blocked by a heap of provisions that had not yet been stowed in its proper location. In the middle of one passageway he encountered three huge green iron oxygen cylinders; each was sealed with a lead wire

87

cap and a stern warning that they were replacements for the tanks aboard the supply tug only. The cylinders were heavy and coated with dust from long storage.

At last Tim found the capsules, tiny counterparts of the green cast-iron giants Ross had seen.

"I'll just give Martino a few minutes of pure O_2 from these tomorrow morning and we'll be ready to go."

"Go? You mean—?" Ross said hesitantly.

"To Main Station," Tim said with a slight lift to his voice. "Commander Keough approved my request to reschedule the supply tug."

"That's really great. How did you talk her into it?"

"I didn't," Tim replied. "She decided that Martino should have his wrist x-rayed on Main Station, and all of a sudden the tug was available."

They walked back to the dispensary. All around them the silent station echoed the sound of their footsteps as they walked down the deserted and half-lighted corridors.

Martino had dozed off in their absence. He was beginning to snore peacefully as Tim put the capsules in his desk and closed the drawer as quietly as he could. Something made him hesitate. He pulled the drawer open and started rummaging through its contents.

"That's odd," he said in an agitated tone of voice.

He went through the sheaf of papers twice. There was a worried expression on his face when he stopped. He pushed the drawer shut and turned and looked at Ross.

"It's gone," Tim whispered.

"What do you mean?"

"Jonathan Hanks's letter isn't where I left it. I hid it underneath the manuscript of my book. While we were in the central storage area someone unlocked the drawer, searched through my correspondence and the manuscript, and stole the letter."

The next twenty-hours were a mixture of frenzied activity broken by stretches of boredom and apathy that began with Ross's futile attempt at a night of solid

88

sleep. He tossed about restlessly until the alarm jolted him from a shallow slumber to the listless awareness of a new morning on *Boreas* station. It continued while he rushed around, madly dressing and packing, then dashed to the galley for a fast and unsatisfying breakfast before the tug was due to cast off.

He was the last to board after saying farewell to Dr. Nystrom and Joel Colbert who were remaining behind; both Tim and Julian Martino were awaiting his arrival. The airlock slammed shut, the rockets burst into a throaty roar, and they were on their way at last.

At once the journey became tedious. The novelty of space flight had worn thin for Ross and Tim, and they both counted the hours remaining with irritated impatience. Ross discovered that his anticipation had been dulled to nothingness by lack of sleep, and Tim appeared equally weary and haggard. Even the prospect of seeing Christy again failed to cheer him and Ross was sure the loss of Hanks's letter weighed heavily on him. Indeed, from time to time Ross saw his friend glance suspiciously in the direction of Julian Martino.

But the assistant, who seemed surprisingly rested and fit for a man recovering from a serious bout with radiation poisoning, easily evaded Tim's eyes. Martino took a great interest in the progress of the flight, hovering by a window and watching the stars slide past. As the hours lengthened the silence within the cabin thickened unbearably around the three passengers, until Martino casually announced that Main Station was in sight.

It was like a reprieve from purgatory. The quiet was broken and the unspoken hostility Ross had been noticing for hours suddenly evaporated as the three of them crowded around the window for their first glimpse of the big metal city turning in the darkness over the Earth. Almost before they were aware of it, the computer piloting the tug made its final course adjustments. And then they were in the hub, approaching the docking collar.

Christy was waiting for them when the airlock doors rolled back. She gave Ross a quick, affectionate hug, then turned to Tim with a kiss that seemed to last forever.

"Glad to see both of you again," she said with a wide smile, her eyes bright and shining happily. "The party here has just started—you two look as though you could use some celebrating."

"Happy New Year," Tim said. "Actually I'm more hungry. The restaurants haven't been closed down for the holiday, have they?"

"Not likely. There's a little place around the corner I know."

"Lead on," Ross said.

"Around the corner" turned out to be a half-mile trek down the crowded corridors of Main Station. And true to her word, the restaurant was small—not much more than an alcove with cafe tables—and brimming full with partying shuttle pilots, maintenance personnel, scientists, secretaries, and administrators of the ISA. Tim groaned.

"Oh, it's usually this jammed," Christy told him. She handed a stub to the headwaiter and said, "But we have reservations."

They were escorted to a table in the center of the room. A waiter took their orders and disappeared into the crowd, and Ross wondered if he would ever find their table again. The restaurant was swarming with visitors, every table occupied with groups of young men and women dressed in the grays and whites of the ISA or decked out in more colorful leisure attire.

"Looks like the assembled multitude on Judgment Day," Ross said, surveying the cafe.

"Everybody's here," Christy replied. "Everybody who could wangle a leave of absence or a pass or the price of a shuttle flight up from Earth started arriving yesterday. I've never seen so many people on Main Station at one time."

At the bar a cluster of off-duty shuttle pilots clad in black suits and silver belts were swapping tales of their latest exploits; nearby, several newly arrived tourists were listening to the banter in stunned astonishment.

Ross spotted a familiar face enter the restaurant, and he rose and went over to greet him.

"Happy New Year, Dr. Ahn," he said.

"Oh. Hello, Ross." Dr. Ahn bowed slightly from the waist. He explained that he was scouting the possibilities of establishing a small research installation on Main Station for the U.S. Air Force.

"Much red tape involved, what you call the 'old runaround.'"

"You get used to that up here," Ross replied. "It seems to be a part of life."

"So true, so true," said Dr. Ahn. "But I do not mind it, because coming to Main Station now gives one a chance to get away from Earth's troubles. You can celebrate. All the men and women here are not in a hurry to return."

"You mean the squabble between China and Australia? I heard the UN settled that."

Dr. Ahn nodded gravely. "The two sides have been negotiating for several months. Just before I depart for Main Station I hear that the talks broke down. Both countries will not back down—will not compromise. They are bringing their people home."

"I didn't know that," said Ross. And it was true, for the events on Earth were of smaller importance to him since he had left it for space. They were distant happenings, somehow unconnected to his life and work on *Boreas* station. But now, he realized, what was happening between the two proud and fearful countries might have a profound effect.

"What do you think will happen?" he asked Dr. Ahn

"What can happen? The Chinese need room to expand, to send their hungry people. Australia has the open land, but refuses to let them in. Both sides have reached an impasse. It is either fight or surrender. And they will not surrender, either of them."

"In a week or so, I think, we will see," he said. "Meanwhile, there is no cause to be glum. There is plenty to keep us active. I especially want to extend

91

holiday greetings to Dr. Nystrom, but I see that it is time for an official conference."

"Dr. Nystrom's not here, anyway."

"So I see," Dr. Ahn said, digging in his coat pocket. He held out a small metal box sealed with black plastic tape. "This is for him. A present for the holidays. Six infrared photographic plates of a very new design. Very, very sensitive; enough to catch the final traces of the radiation from the nova he told me he was studying so intently. Do you know when he will return?"

"Return?" Ross said in a puzzled voice.

"Yes, for I would like to present these plates to him myself," the Korean scientist replied.

"I don't think you understand," Ross said. "Dr. Nystrom is on *Boreas* station. He stayed behind to finish up his work."

Dr. Ahn's jaw dropped in surprise.

"But that cannot be so."

"It is. Only one tug flight was run between *Boreas* and Main Station. Julian Martino, Tim, and I were the only ones aboard it, I'm absolutely sure."

"That is impossible, Ross. I saw him ten minutes ago in the hallway outside this restaurant!"

CHAPTER TEN

The two men regarded one another for a few silent moments. The hubbub of the restaurant seemed to diminish in Ross's ears as he considered Dr. Ahn's statement.

"I don't see how that could be," Ross finally said.

"You are sure?" asked the diminutive Asian, his voice almost plaintive.

"Positive," Ross replied firmly. "There's only a limited number of tugs to begin with, and they're all tied up over the holidays. If Dr. Nystrom did not ride here on the tug I used—and I'm certain he didn't—he must still be on *Boreas*. There is no way he could get here."

Dr. Ahn froze. Then, a sudden flash of realization seemed to cross his features and he said hastily, "Of course you are correct; how foolish of me not to understand! I must have been mistaken, the man I saw could not have been Dr. Nystrom. That is the only rational explanation, is it not?"

Ross agreed, but he also found himself with a vague sense of doubt. He had a slight lingering suspicion that Dr. Ahn was too quick to admit his error, for some inexplicable reason.

"Alas," said Dr. Ahn, peering at his wristwatch. "I shall be late for my conference. I am given to understand that Mr. Gurvich is not one to be kept waiting. Because I may not meet you again before you depart, might I entrust you with the film for Dr. Nystrom, please? I would appreciate it most gratefully."

He appeared anxious to be on his way, so Ross accepted the metal container and promised to relay it to Dr. Nystrom on his return to *Boreas* station. Dr. Ahn mumbled his thanks and withdrew from the restaurant, leaving Ross with the film and an uneasy feeling of suspicion.

But as he wended his way back through the holiday crowd to his table, he decided the incident was too trivial for further discussion and he met the quizzical stares of Christy and Tim with a neutral shrug of his shoulders.

It didn't work.

"He's onto something," Tim said to Christy as Ross sat down across from them.

"How can you tell?" she replied.

"Oh, I know when something is brewing beneath that calm exterior," Tim said lightly. "Come on, Ross, what's happening?"

"Why all the sudden curiosity?"

"Just a hunch," Tim replied. "You look perturbed."

"It's nothing. Nothing at all," Ross assured Tim.

"Don't bother about him," Christy said to Ross. "Tim's gotten so wrapped up with detective stories recently I think he's fallen into thinking he's one himself."

"Not so!" said Tim insistently, but still only half-serious. "I finished writing the book last week; that mystery is over. But I'm really intrigued by this new one."

Ross had to smile. "I just told you, Sherlock, it's nothing more than a case of mistaken identity. Dr. Ahn apparently saw somebody here on Main Station who resembled Dr. Nystrom. All I did was tell him Dr. Nystrom was working on Boreas right now."

Christy opened her mouth to speak, but at that moment their waiter arrived with a trayful of food. As the man proceeded around the table, setting down the plates and bowls and tureens and silverware, Ross recalled Dr. Nystrom's caution against elaborate synthesized dishes. Now, he thought, the warning came just a little late. Ross looked doubtfully at his order, a steaming serving of deliciously fragrant Creole shrimp piled high on his platter.

It smelled wonderful and appeared as real and natural as the New Orleans original: succulent white shrimp and a thick pale pink sauce over long grains of wild rice. It was far and away the most convincing imitation Ross had ever encountered. He speared a shrimp on the tip of his fork and, with only a bit of trepidation, he investigated further.

"Say, this is marvelous," he said happily. "The chemists must be working overtime."

Without further hesitation Ross devoured his meal, making a mental note to tell Dr. Nystrom about the vast culinary advances being made here. The big astronomer probably would be delighted to learn he could safely abandon his cheese omelet for a variety of dishes, Ross thought, cleaning his plate and looking forward with anticipation to dessert.

After the meal, Christy got up from the table.

"I think I'm going to change," she announced.

"Don't do it!" Tim said, the faintest smile on his face. "I rather like the shape you have right now."

"All right," she replied, playing along. "I'll keep *that*. But the clothes must go—the party's due to start and I don't wish to be seen in this lab coat and these stuffy white shoes. Makes me feel really ancient."

"Oh, you look fine," Tim said. "However, I can tell by the look on your face I'll never properly convince you of that. Well, I'll meet you there."

"Keep your eyes wide open, then, 'cause you probably won't ever recognize me." She turned away, toward the door.

"I'll find you," Tim called to her. "Somehow."

Ross guessed that the last word was drowned in the incessant din of the restaurant, but that didn't seem to bother Tim. He watched Christy disappear into a throng of tourists waiting for tables by the entrance.

He sighed. "Isn't she sensational?" he asked Ross.

"Very. You're really lucky, you know."

"Best thing that ever happened to me, I think."

"How did you first meet her?" Ross asked.

"We were in the same classes at medical school for two years running," Tim replied, his voice gentle, remembering. "Those were two great years. Of all the students in our classes she had the most spirit. Nothing fazed Christine Reney. She was the only one who didn't turn green when they wheeled the cadaver into the anatomy class for dissection."

"Sounds wonderful."

"Sorry, Ross. I got carried away. Anyhow, she decided to go into research, while I opted for general practice. The result was we sort of drifted apart, and it was only when she came to work on Main Station that we started getting together again. I had forgotten, a little, just how special she was. As it is I miss her terribly when she's away—"

"Like now?"

Slowly Tim nodded in agreement, then said, "But this one time I'm glad she decided to leave for a while. When you went over to talk to Dr. Ahn, I got a call from Jonathan Hanks. He wanted to talk to me."

"Alone?"

"No. I let him know that you also have the information in the letter,"

"Have you told Christy what the contents of his letter was?" Ross said.

Tim shook his head.

"Then she doesn't know, either, that it's been stolen from your desk?"

"That's right. I've avoided the entire subject when I'm with her. I don't want her to know what Hanks uncovered," said Tim in a low, controlled voice. It was nearly a whisper.

"Are you afraid of her finding out anyway?"

"Yeah. A little. Because I don't even know what it

all *means,* but I know it means something. Commander Keough and Julian Martino didn't decide for nothing to obscure part of their collective past, I'm sure. It's not a game with them; they don't play games."

"I'm fully aware of that fact," Ross replied. "But don't you think they might be acting out of some minor motive? Maybe it enables them to cheat on their income tax."

Tim almost laughed, but the serious tone in his voice returned in a moment.

"Touché! That consideration had crossed my mind at the beginning of this affair. It crossed pretty fast. Look at what they're risking, Ross. If the two of them are found out, under the bylaws of the ISA charter they'll lose their jobs. And their professional reputations, too. There would be enormous repercussions in the ISA and in the military if Keough and Martino were exposed."

"Do you really believe those events would take place?"

"Of course there's a lot at stake here. More than we know—probably more than we *want* to know," said Tim. "And because of that I don't want Christy involved. She could get hurt, and it would be my fault for it happening. No. I've made my mind up, Christy keeps out of this mess entirely."

"An admirable course of action," said a gravel-toned voice behind Ross. Ross swung around, startled, to face the source of that gruff statement.

Jonathan Hanks was as lean and as lank as Ross remembered him being months ago on *Boreas* station. His hair was a trifle longer and less kempt, his electrician's overalls were not so flashy as his previous outfit and his left arm was encased in a shiny rigid tube of poured plastic.

Otherwise he was just the same.

"Good move," he told Tim as he sat down at their table. "A conspiracy should always have as few members as possible."

Ross blanched. He was sure that every single person

97

in the restaurant had heard Hanks's remark. One thing Hanks possessed above all else was a clear and resounding bass, the kind, Ross thought with an inward groan, that carries and carries and carries. However, a few furtive glances at the holiday crowd seemed to indicate that no one had been listening. Or if so, the remark would have been taken as a good-natured joke. Which it was, in a way.

Hanks dropped into his chair. "New Year, gentlemen," he said warmly.

"And the same," Tim replied, staring at Hanks's left arm. "How did that happen?"

"My busted wing? Conduit fell atop me," Hanks said.

"It's been a bad year for left arms," Ross said. Tim nodded vigorously.

"Ah, the thing's no more than an inconvenience. Got the medic a little worried though. Put me in a nice comfortable bed in one of the wards for a day to be sure I had no other internal injuries. I had none."

"But—but you never even mentioned your injury in that letter," Tim said.

"Like I say, it's a thing of small consequence." Hanks shrugged his shoulders. "And I had other things taking up my attention. Such as the other fellow in my ward. The medics called him Winters, but I thought I'd met him before. For the longest spell I couldn't place him. Then I recalled, back then his name was Thorton. An electronics specialist, working on *Boreas* station when it was assembled. Five years ago.

"Well," Hanks continued, "I got interested and struck up a conversation. This Thorton character had himself a job on the *Basketball* using the name Winters. He told me his job was seeing to patching the leaky seams on that old gasbag."

"What's wrong with that?" Ross said.

"Just this; what's a high talent specialist like Thorton doing claiming his name is something else and his occupation is manual labor only the most menial space-jack gets assigned? And this "Winters" didn't know the first thing about spacesuits, either. He's spent his working days in his shirtsleeves. Lying all the way, he was. And to top it off, he tried to pass off a microtorch burn as a severe sunburn!"

"What's a microtorch man doing on a satellite like the Basketball?" Ross wondered aloud. "Microtorching is used to fabricate elaborate electronic components."

"That's it," Hanks fairly shouted, then lowered his voice.

"That's nothing," Tim said. "He might have been assembling a radio or TV receiver for the crew."

"I have my doubts. Equipment like that would be delivered to the Basketball in one unit. No, microtorching is for large operations. And Thorton's been working on the Basketball for months. I checked his file."

"Doesn't make any sense," Tim said. "None of it does, except for one item. A lot of people are lying."

"And getting away with it," Ross said. "Nobody in the ISA seems to care."

"That's what I think, too," said Hanks. "What are we going to do about it?"

"What can we do?" Tim asked.

"Go to Gurvich," said Ross, "and tell him what we all have found out. He's the director of operations for the ISA. He will listen, I'll bet."

"I'm not so sure of that approach," Hanks cautioned. "If we're wrong, if it all turns out to be perfectly legitimate, we all are cooked. We still don't know enough to make a case."

"You can't sit on top of this kind of information forever," replied Ross, finding himself suddenly agitated. His throat was dry and his heart was beating hard in his chest.

'I don't think forever will be necessary, Ross. Just a while more. I'm finished up here on Main, this busted wing sees to that. I'm supposed to be on the next shuttle to London, tomorrow," Hanks said.

"That shoots everything," Tim said despondently.

"Oh, not at all," Hanks replied. "I'l send you my address. You two, in turn, keep your ears open to things—rumors and gossip and small talk—and if anything of substance comes of it, let me know. I'll check it out, and then submit a full report to the ISA." Hanks looked at each of them. "Will you agree to that, at least?"

They agreed. Reluctantly.

"I still feel like we should take action now. The time is right," Ross said. "The ISA would be forced to investigate. In a month or two, all our information will be cold."

"Believe me," Hanks said. "If anything suspicious is happening, the ISA will move—and quickly. It may be a bureaucracy, but I think it will react if the evidence is there in plain sight."

Ross was still dubious; however, he was beginning to realize that Hanks's plan was the one with the best chance of success. He saw that a rash action might endanger them all in some unsuspected way. All three of them, he clearly recognized, would have to be alert from this moment on.

"It's settled, then?" Tim said shakily. "Good. The party should be starting up right about now, and I think it's high time we had some fun!"

Nobody disagreed with that suggestion, and the three of them wandered over to the auditorium where the New Year's party was noisily in progress. By the time they arrived a huge crowd had accumulated and spilled out into the hallway. From within Ross could hear the steady, insistent beat of a dance band and the bright sounds of laughter floating in the air.

The lights were very low and growing dimmer as they entered.

"I can't see anybody," Hanks said over the level of the music that was pouring from a stack of speakers at the far end of the room.

"Neither can I," Ross said. "But I think that's the point."

"Right," added Tim, clapping to the music. "It's every man for himself from now on."

Hours had passed.

That much Ross knew. He wasn't sure how many, and it really didn't seem to matter. The band was still going strong, playing set after set until Ross wondered if they weren't humans after all, but talented and tireless robots perched up on that makeshift stage amid the white clouds of smoke.

The idea amused him for awhile, and he realized he was getting lightheaded. Whether it was the effect of the party punch or the acrid sting of the cigarettes or the lights or the endless and hypnotic music he never knew or cared. He was quite happy with the way things were.

He was dancing with an extraordinarily attractive young woman, one of the stewardesses on the shuttle run. She was wearing an outfit that glinted in the phosphorescent orange and emerald spotlights like a shower of sparks every time she moved. Which was often, Ross observed, and very well, too. He wondered what her name was and was on the point of inquiring when two events occurred in rapid succession.

The wide, quicksilvery smile on the stewardess's lips vanished and her eyes turned away from his. Then Ross felt the slightest feather touch of a hand on his shoulder, tapping insistently. It was as if a live wire had brushed his skin. He spun around.

It was another girl, a bit taller than the stewardess. This one, though, was dressed all in gray velvet that exactly matched her eyes. Gray eyes. Gray eyes and a fall of blonde hair. And with that, recognition came to him.

"Christy!" Ross exclaimed. "You look dazzling."

She smiled. "I'm glad you like the dress, Ross, but I didn't come looking for you just to show off. Tim and I've been searching the station for you."

"I have been right here."

"So I see. I really hate to break this up," Christy said to Ross. "But I have to tell you something."

"Can't it wait?"

"I'm afraid not. Tim found out an hour ago that both of you have to go back immediately. Your leave's been canceled."

"Oh, no! There must be a mistake."

She shook her head.

"There isn't. The order came through about an hour ago," Christy replied. "We were standing around the punchbowl talking to some of my friends, when Julian Martino walked up and gave Tim his leave cancellation."

Ross felt a sudden rage when he heard that name spoken. "So he did it!" Ross said bitterly. "That's typical of his style, can't stand to see people enjoying themselves. He has to cut it off, throw his weight around—"

Christy held up her hand. "Wait a minute."

There was a second of silence. They were standing outside the auditorium now, the band had stopped for a rest, and Ross could hear the next words Christy said with absolute clarity.

"Martino didn't order the tug back to *Boreas,* Ross, and neither did Eva Keough. Tim thought the same way you did. But he was wrong, too; somebody else turned in the request to recall the tug."

"Who then?" Ross said, snapping irritably. "Whose fault was it?"

"Dr. Nystrom." She paused. "He asked for the leave cancellation and signed the orders. It's his fault, if you want to call it that."

Tim and Julian Martino soon were shutting the airlock after they boarded the tug. Twenty minutes later the tug was deep in space.

CHAPTER ELEVEN

"Dead? Are you certain?"

On *Boreas* station the scheduled, artificial night still had several hours remaining before the ceiling lights were restored to their full intensity. Ross's question seemed to hang, quivering, in the somber labyrinth of the radio astronomy lab.

"I am certain of it," replied Dr. Nystrom's voice. It echoed faintly.

"But . . . how?" said Tim a moment later.

Dr. Nystrom scratched the back of his hand idly before he answered.

"I really have no idea why the relay satellite suddenly ceased transmitting," he said finally. "One instant it was actively radioing a normal flow of data from the Earth station. Then the telemetry stopped. It was totally silent. I couldn't detect *any* signals. Even the carrier waves were dead."

"Couldn't the trouble have been a burnt-out transistor, or something like that?" Ross asked.

Dr. Nystrom handed both of them a bulb of coffee and said, "That's what I thought at first. A minor malfunction. But the relay was designed with all its systems in parallel, so if one failed, a duplicate could take over the load. No, whatever happened involved the whole mechanism.

"Then, I panicked," Dr. Nystrom went on, reddening

with embarrassment. "I simply had to have that data to wrap up my observations of the nova. As soon as I found there was no hope of reviving the satellite, I went straight to Commander Keough and demanded the use of the tug so I could go check on it myself. I couldn't think of anything else, except finding out what went wrong. I didn't realize, then, my actions would drag you both back here. Please accept my apologies."

Whatever resentment he still felt seemed to exaporate when Ross heard that admission: *I panicked.* Considering the circumstances, Ross thought, it was a completely understandable reaction. I wonder if I would have responded any differently? he asked himself.

"Put it out of your mind," Ross said mildly to Dr. Nystrom. "The party was getting to be kind of a drag, anyway."

He and Tim instinctively realized that this was a far more serious matter, and they found their thoughts and conversation returning to it shortly.

"The only thing I don't like," Tim said, "is your insistence to go it alone from here on. Piloting that tug is no simple operation, I understand."

"It's not for amateurs, I agree. But I think I can handle it by myself, Tim, since most of the controls and the primary guidance systems are computerized. Why, I imagine you could handle the tug satisfactorily in an emergency."

"I would like to try," Tim replied. "Besides, that is exactly what I meant, what does happen to you, alone, in an emergency situation?"

"I would try to work it out on my own," Dr. Nystrom said, musing.

"Two people would work it out faster," Ross added.

"Perhaps. However, if that were the case I wouldn't like to be responsible for another's life; all in all, it's less complicated my way. And what is this gloomy talk about emergencies, anyway? I have complete faith in the equipment I'll be using."

"The relay satellite failed," Ross said.

"Only because a man wasn't aboard it," Dr. Nystrom

countered. "Somebody wasn't there to see the trouble develop and take steps to correct it. A machine can't make those kind of decisions and observations, but a human being can.

"No," he said, continuing, "as soon as the tug is refueled and readied I'll be off to collect my errant little satellite in person."

"That may be a while longer," Ross told him. He explained that on their return trip to *Boreas* station, they had inadvertently found that the amount of breathable oxygen stored on the tug had diminished to a dangerously low level because the vessel had been in nearly continuous use. "When the tug docked here there was about three hours' supply remaining. Tim filled out a requisition to have new tanks installed in the tug, drawn from a stockpile in central storage."

"Thanks," said Dr. Nystrom. "That was good work on your part. Now I only hope the additional delay won't add too many more hours to the search plan."

The complexities of the transorbital flight Dr. Nystrom had mapped out allowed little leeway. Intercepting the relay satellite would require an almost incredible coordination of fuel expenditure, velocity, and direction to arrive at the same speed and altitude of the relay at the precise second of the satellite's passage. The fact that the relay no longer transmitted radio signals added another complication; any final locating would require some intricate "blind" navigating with the tug's radar system. Estimated flight time, from departure and descent to a low orbit to retrieve the relay and then return to *Boreas* station, was seventy-four hours.

"And every minute spent waiting here means a correspondingly greater number tacked on later," Dr. Nystrom grumbled, but it was clear that he was looking forward to the flight with ill-disguised enthusiasm. His large and robust frame was clothed in a light blue coverall, a comfortable garment durable enough to last the duration of the voyage without developing annoying wrinkles next to the skin. It would also provide a good

105

insulating layer should the radio astronomer have to don a spacesuit quickly. He fidgeted several more minutes, then announced he was going to the tug.

"I think I had better see what this holdup's about," he said, gathering up three large bundles and heading for the door with Ross and Tim close behind.

"You're traveling light for three days away," Ross said, watching him tow the suitcases along.

"Socks and underwear in one, a stack of technical journals in the second," came the reply. "My reading has been piling up at an alarming rate since *Nova Aurigae* flared up. What with all those empty hours ahead, I'll have time enough to catch up."

Soon they had turned a corner and were standing before the entryway to the tug's command section. No one else was in sight, but Ross could hear the sounds of doors rolling shut toward the aft end of the vessel.

"Still working," Dr. Nystrom said with a resigned sigh. "I can't believe it's taking this long."

Ross glanced at his watch. "Only been an hour and a half since Tim and I pulled in. I'm sure maintenance knows you're in a hurry."

"Probably right, I shouldn't grouse. Especially since I'll be gone long enough, anyway."

"I'm surprised you secured permission to have the station's only tug at your disposal for three days," Tim said.

"Oh, I doubt it'll throw the schedule of operations off by much," replied Dr. Nystrom. He seemed to be closely following the various mechanical noises emanating from the tug's interior.

"What I mean is that you managed to talk Eva Keough into releasing the tug to you, you alone."

"I didn't have to talk her into it," said Dr. Nystrom. "When I asked her to recall the tug from Main Station she agreed readily."

"And you don't consider that surprising?"

"No, Why should it be?"

Tim paused a moment.

"I'm not actually sure," he said slowly. "Just that it

106

seems strange, to me at least, that she would be so willing to grant your wishes. You two haven't been the best of friends, you know."

"That is very true," said Dr. Nystrom. "Nevertheless, the fact stands that she did arrange for the tug to be returned."

"Sure enough. Maybe the commander is coming around to your point of view. That would be nice, for a change."

"Yes, it would. Somehow, though, I don't think that's what she had in mind, Tim. I rather imagine she saw this as an opportunity to temporarily get me out of her hair, so to speak."

"That's awful," Ross said.

"You may consider that a cynical thing to say," Dr. Nystrom replied evenly. "I have known the commander for some time now, and I can understand her motives a bit better. When I went to her office with my request, she appeared deep in thought about some other matter, and doubtless I jostled her from her thoughts enough to annoy her into sending for the tug—if only to get me away."

He smiled. "I recall that she seemed taken aback when I broached the subject, but it took her only a moment to approve the request. Then she hustled me out the door and shut it firmly behind me."

Disappointment showed in Tim's expression, Ross thought, and also in the young doctor's voice when at last he spoke.

"And here I thought you and she were on the verge of patching up your differences," Tim said. *"Boreas* station could stand some harmony and peace after all these tense months."

"It would have been a beneficial gesture," Dr. Nystrom said, nodding in agreement. "If only that had been the intent of the commander's actions. But wait, while I'm gone—and if the atmosphere around here *does* relax due to my absence—there's no reason you couldn't try to reconcile your differences with her."

"I don't know—" Tim said dubiously.

"Come on, Tim," said Dr. Nystrom with an infectious, encouraging grin. "I realize you and Eva Keough don't see eye to eye, but you could change that—a little, at least. It might calm some of the antagonism here, and you must admit you just said that would be pleasant."

"I did. But it would take a miracle to make *Boreas* a friendly place. I think Commander Keough likes it the way it is now. After all, she's made little attempt to change it."

Dr. Nystrom nodded quietly.

"Perhaps it is wishful thinking," he said. "Yet I feel that she's actually a decent human being. Only something has forced her to become the way she is, something hidden deep inside her. If that could be broken, altered—"

They were silent for a while.

Dr. Nystrom looked at Ross and Tim, then said: "Probably you are right; probably it's simply wishful thinking on my part. But it's worth trying, if only once. If the opportunity comes, how terrible it would be to waste it."

The noises from the tug's aft had ceased, and a second later the loudspeaker reported that the vessel was prepared for its long loop around the Earth and back.

Tossing his two suitcases into the cockpit, Dr. Nystrom extended his hand to shake all around before clambering up the entranceway and into the tug.

"I'll see what can be done about your suggestion," Tim promised.

"Do try," Dr. Nystrom called back. He was hunched over the main control panel, busily punching in flight data to the tug's computer, and his voice carried badly. "Would be a fine thing to return to."

Warning signs flashed around the docking collar and the forward hatch was inching closed when Ross was struck by a sudden realization.

"Hey," he shouted into the entryway as loud as he

could, "what will happen to Whit for the time you're gone?"

In the turn of events, Dr. Nystrom's pet had been completely overlooked, until now.

From within the fore end of the tug came the unmistakable sound of a chuckle. The closing of the hatch was halted momentarily.

Dr. Nystrom's voice boomed out. "Why, nothing at all, Ross. You see, I couldn't bear to leave him on *Boreas*. Whit's accompanying me on this expedition."

"Where is he, then?"

"Here." Ross saw, though the crack that remained open, the lid of the third parcel, a wicker box, open to release a tiny, swift, darting thing into the air. "See. Your fears were groundless. I'm not traveling alone!"

CHAPTER TWELVE

When Ross woke the next morning he could hardly move. Six hours earlier he had fallen asleep to the purring of the air duct over his bunk; now it seemed to roar like a waterfall in his aching ears. His joints were stiff and painful, he discovered, and his stomach rumbled threateningly when he tried to sit up. After listlessly dressing, he headed automatically to the galley for breakfast.

The smell of food hit him as he walked through the door. It was like the wind off a stockyard, thick and hot and nauseating. At once, everything began thrashing and churning inside him, down and up and down again. Ross's head started spinning wildly.

He fled to the dispensary.

Luckily Tim was there already, shelving a box of pharmaceuticals. He took one look at Ross and stuck a thermometer under his tongue for a second until it registered.

"One hundred degrees even," Tim pronounced shortly, peering closely at the plastic spiral clenched between Ross's teeth. He ran though a short list of symptoms, item by item. At the end, Tim leaned forward in his chair and rested his elbows on the shiny top of the desk.

"Intestinal influenza virus," Tim said. "Plain old stomach flu is the culprit."

That made sense, Ross thought, feeling his insides attempt to rearrange themselves. "I've never had it. Bad?"

"That depends. Eaten anything?"

Ross groaned at the thought and vigorously shook his head.

"That makes the cure much simpler," said Tim. He went into the station's compact but highly efficient pharmacy for a minute, returning with a clear plastic bottle half-filled with enormous white capsules. "Take one now, another in an hour."

Ross hesitated, then gulped down the pill. His stomach reacted savagely until the prescription started to have its desired effect. "That's much better, thanks," Ross said gratefully, feeling the pain begin to ebb from his shoulders and back.

"You probably contracted that particular virus at the party on Main Station," Tim said. "Lot of people wandering around from Earth there. It's fortunate you developed it after the trip back, and not during—"

Ross blocked the image from his mind. "What now?" he said in a voice that sounded more like a croak.

"You're off the 'Active' list for twenty-four hours so you don't pass along your bug to the rest of *Boreas*. Now back to bed; I'll see you later when I make my rounds."

"Your rounds? Who else has the flu?"

"Nobody, yet," Tim replied. "I have to make sure Julian Martino gets his antiradiation injections to stop the poisoning he received in the reactor accident. I wish I could persuade Commander Keough to transfer him to the hospital on Main, there he could get the rest and care he should have."

"Why don't you simply *order* him moved?"

Tim shook his head in exasperation. "He wants to stay here, as well as the commander. That's stiff opposition. Julian Martino isn't being transferred anywhere."

All that morning and through the afternoon Ross slept fitfully, dozing and waking every so often, occas-

111

ionally swallowing another white capsule. Time seemed to be elastic, now rushing past him, now creeping along.

Very dimly he was aware of the routine of work taking place beyond the narrow cubicle he was now occupying, but it meant nothing to him, nor did the appearance of a friendly face at the door now and then. It was more like a dream of something he had known and forgotten, and the hours lengthened and were transformed into a warm flowing lassitude. Ross felt as though a tropical current was washing over him. Wave followed wave in a gentle irresistible tide . . .

And he slept once again.

Hands were shaking him, jostling his shoulders. Not roughly, and certainly not soothingly, observed part of his consciousness. They were purposeful, those hands. But what purpose could there be?

To wake up fully, came the unspoken reply from another part of his brain. They want to wake you up.

Ross opened his eyes, blinking at the sharp, sudden glare in his eyes. The hands stopped shaking him, and in a moment he heard the murmuring of voices.

"Ross," someone was saying. "Ross."

The voice turned away. "He's not responding," it said.

"The effect of those capsules should have worn off by now," replied a second voice, coming closer. "Ross! Wake up, Ross!"

An image swam before his eyes, steadied.

"Tim, what's all the racket?" Ross said in a surprisingly clear voice. "What's going on here?"

There was a chattering multitude of voices, all at once. Ross sat up. His room was full of people. Tim, of course, was standing nearby. The Colberts were there, also, looking at him with concerned expressions on their faces. Near the door was another figure, dressed in a dark uniform. It was Commander Eva Keough.

"Ross, can you hear me OK?" Tim said, bending over him slightly.

112

"Of course I can," Ross replied, a slight trace of annoyance in his voice. "Do you think I've gone deaf?"

"The medicine you've been taking is pretty potent stuff. I wasn't sure you weren't still groggy."

"Just sleepy. I feel fine now," Ross said. He indicated the gathering with a sweep of his hand. "You holding a wake for me? Strange duty for a doctor."

"I try to anticipate every possible circumstance," Tim said, smiling. "There's a reason for the get-together, all right, and believe me I wouldn't have roused you this early if it wasn't a good reason."

Tim stepped out of the way and Commander Keough walked up to the edge of the bunk.

"Do you think you will be able to get up and walk around soon, Mr. Moran?" she asked him in a pleasant voice.

"Just allow me a minute to change into my clothes," Ross said.

"That is excellent. I hoped you might be recovered enough by now."

The way she phrased her sentences gave them an ominous ring and Ross felt compelled to ask what was going wrong.

"Here—nothing whatsoever. However, on Earth the situation is different. One of the commercial passenger shuttles was forced to make an emergency crash landing in the Arctic Ocean north of Canada."

"Any survivors?"

"No one knows," Commander Keough said. "All contact with the shuttle stopped midway through reentry into the atmosphere when its rocket engine exploded. The craft was thrown into a divergent path of descent and is presumed to have impacted in the vicinity of Meighen Island."

The Arctic Ocean north of Canada. A memory floated to the surface of his thoughts.

"The storm," he said. "Wasn't a storm building in the Arctic? I recall shooting some cassettes of the leading edge of the low pressure movement."

For the first time so far, Joel Colbert began speak-

113

ing. Quickly he outlined the development and course the storm was taking as it spread across the frozen seas. It was a terrifying picture of Nature at its cruelest: gale-driven winds, jagged ice particles swept down from clouds the color of lead, utter cold penetrating to the marrow of the bone, and a brilliant blinding whiteness in all directions.

"They crashed in *that?*" Ross said, incredulous, shaking his head in fearful wonder.

"Yes, they crashed into the storm itself," replied Commander Keough. "A ground rescue is being organized, but it will be handicapped because the specific location of the crash is not known. A rough estimate is all we have to work from."

"We?"

"The ISA has assigned *Boreas* the job of finding the spot where the shuttle went down," Myra Colbert said. "Joel and I have done some of the preliminary scanning already, but the task is too big for just the two of us."

"And you want me to help, too?" Ross said.

"That is the point of this meeting," Commander Keough said. "It is a request, not an order."

"All right," said Ross immediately. "When do we start?"

"As soon as you can report to the turret and activate the cameras, Mr. Moran."

After eight days the monster was still growing, bulging to the south and east with frightening energy. Distance meant nothing to the storm. Its icewinds spanned the arctic sea like the legs of a living being, its feet brushed the surface with powerful, ponderous strides, its body all cloud and snow and dark freezing air a dozen miles high. It was almost alive, Ross thought as he saw it again though his cameras, this polar nightmare.

And somewhere in the vast and bleak maw of this storm lay an insignificant chip of metal.

Somewhere. Ten hours of observation had not yet

114

found it, though the search was pressed to the utmost now. The storm had hidden its captives well.

If there were captives. Ross, seeing straight into the bitter center of the storm, was doubtful that survivors still lived. It was beyond belief that human beings could endure exposure to the relentless hostility on the surface without special protection from the chilling winds. The broken hull of the shuttle, Ross thought grimly, would hardly provide adequate shelter for anyone fortunate enough to live through the disaster.

"Anything?" said Myra Colbert over the intercom.

"Negative," Ross told her after rechecking his work of the past two hours once more. "Still no letup in the area around Meighen Island. In fact, it looks worse than before. I don't understand how a ground rescue team could get through."

"The charted windspeed in that vicinity is one hundred miles an hour," Myra Colbert said after a moment. "No aircraft is going to try to buck those gales."

Silently Ross approved, as the painful memory of another flight into another storm long ago drifted into his thoughts. Enough have died already, he thought. Why should more perish? He could think of no sensible answer.

"It'll have to be a ground search party, then," Ross replied. "They'll have a tough time crossing the ice floes what with the wind drifting and cracking the surface. You'd better advise Earth of that."

"Good point, but I'm not the one to communicate with Earth, Ross. Commander Keough has left instructions that all sightings and observations are to be sent to her office first, and *then* they'll be routed to the ground."

"Sounds to me like a waste of time."

Myra Colbert was patient. "It's simply the way things are. The commander was pretty insistent. She wants to know first off if we spot anything."

"She had better not hold her breath. The storm's worse now than it was on last hour's scan; it just keeps on thickening. I've tried everything I can think of to

115

see the surface, but that cloud layer's blocking each instrument."

Ross paused.

"It's hopeless. I can't make out a single detail. Maybe in one or two days, if the storm settles down a little—"

"Any survivors will be dead," Myra said.

"I know that, but what else is there to do? Those storm clouds are like a concrete wall over the Arctic Ocean. I don't feel very happy admitting defeat, but that's what the situation is. We're licked. We might as well admit it."

"Have you tried everything? How about the infrared 'scope?" said Joel Colbert urgently.

"Right at the beginning. The infrared system is limited to wide-angle shots of general heat flow in the atmosphere. Nothing the size of the shuttle would even register on the film."

Joel Colbert waited for what seemed like an hour before his voice returned, crackling from the speaker.

"If that is so, then I am forced to agree with you. I'll advise the commander right away."

Predictably, Commander Eva Keough was hardly pleased. She greeted the news with irritation, snapping questions at Ross and the Colberts until it seemed to them that she was holding them personally responsible for the storm that was blocking the shuttle crash site. Ross contained his temper and explained his conclusion over again.

"All right," said Commander Keough when he had finished. "I understand that it would be fruitless to continue with your observations at this time. I will radio to Earth authorities and tell them what you have just told me. You three should try to get some rest, for the search will resume in eight hours."

Ross breathed thankfully. He was bone-weary and knew that he wasn't far from complete exhaustion. He craved sleep more than any other thing at that moment, and turned with drowsy anticipation toward the switch that would silence the intercom.

He was reaching for it when Commander Keough

116

broke the quiet in the turret, saying, "This station possesses the most advanced photographic equipment available. So if it cannot locate the shuttle, and some other agency—not as well equipped—does find it, I will be asked many exceedingly difficult questions about the worthiness of the crewmembers under my direction. Let it be hoped that this does not come to pass."

With that warning the intercom clicked off.

Ross returned to his room and sprawled onto his bunk. He lay there, motionless, his body demanding sleep. His mind refused to loosen its grip; it continued to examine his decision to call off the search.

Was it right to stop looking for the crash site? he asked himself. While the possibility existed that people could still be alive down in that howling tempest? Had he done all he could?

Around and around the thoughts spun madly through his conscience, seeking to awaken . . . what?

Something stirred. Ross sat up.

Something in the past, something he had almost forgotten tugged at him and would not go away.

As if they were acting on their own, Ross felt his eyes swivel in the darkened room toward his jacket hung carelessly on a peg in the wall.

Ross got up, crossed the floor, and groped about in the jacket pocket until he found it. His hand closed around it, feeling the cool smooth sides. A small metal container. Dr. Ahn's gift to Dr. Nystrom. The film.

His mind was functioning at a high pitch of excitement, recalling the Korean's words: *six infrared photographic plates of a new design. Very, very sensitive. . . .*

Ross crammed the container into his shirt front and headed out the door. By the time he reached the turret his feet ached from running all the way.

There were six squares of film inside the package, and they fit easily into a frame mount. Ross loaded them into the infrared scanning 'scope, one by one. He shut the loader and entered the turret.

The approximate area of the shuttle crash was still in night, which would help increase the contrast Ross

117

hoped as he aligned the telescope-camera and programmed it to photograph a rectangular grid pattern.

Peering through the viewfinder, Ross could make out no details except a smear of cloud and a tiny portion of Meighen Island. It didn't matter, the infrared film would "see" in its own special way, not the intense darkness of the storm, but varying tones of heat and cold. And, Ross thought, if this stuff is as sensitive as Dr. Ahn said, there was the chance it might possibly detect the residue of heat the shuttle picked up as it plunged through the atmosphere like a guided meteor.

He started the camera.

Rapidly there were six heavy clinking sounds from the telescope. Six exposures, one a second.

The sequence was complete.

The negatives were ejected from the camera. Ross scooped them up into their container and set off for the gravity end of *Boreas* where the auxiliary darkroom was located. He had decided to process the film by hand, rather than trust the work to the machine.

It was finished in a few minutes. Ross slapped the wet negatives down on a glass-topped table. Neon lamps were set below the glass and so provided brilliant ilumination for the films.

The six negatives were startling; swirling bands of gold and scarlet were the images of the atmospheric heat flows over the Arctic Ocean. Stone-cold Meighen Island appeared as a charcoal gray splotch on one of the negatives, and Ross noticed that the details of the Island were exquisite; Dr. Ahn had told him the truth about the extraordinary sensitivity of these films.

They were better than he ever imagined.

They almost seemed magical, for the storm and the snow were gone entirely from the negatives—stripped away—leaving the surface markings clear and recognizable.

The first and the second films revealed nothing out of the ordinary, just the crumpled forms of the ice sheet and the turbulent air above it.

Ross moved on to the third, craning his head and

trying to focus his eyes more sharply. He went through it and was about to set it aside when a yellow point at one edge of the film attracted his attention. He reached for a magnifier.

The point expanded. It was unmistakable: a dart with stubby wings, crimped and splintered to one side but intact and complete. It was resting in a rough oval of what Ross took to be meltwater. The dart was dull yellow, not gray like the island. That meant heat was radiating from it, hours after it had crashed. There still might be life . . .

Frantically Ross jabbed at the intercom switch. The office of the commander did not reply. Then he tried the assistant's office with the same result. Ross snatched up the precious negative and ran out to the central hallway. The lights were dim overhead and there was no sound of voices.

Was everyone asleep on *Boreas* station? he wondered, feeling the emptiness. He started walking to the station's communications center, hoping to meet someone on the way.

The door to the center was closed but not locked. Ross opened it and found that the center was also unoccupied and still, except for the persistent chatter of interstation telemetry.

Ross picked up a microphone and depressed the *transmit* key.

Then he stopped, grasping the wandlike mike in his hand. He was dimly aware that there was some procedure involved—securing authority. Something like that. He yawned sleepily and keyed his call down to Main Station; there an operator patched his line into primary laser link to Earth. In seconds, Ross heard a professional-sounding voice.

"North American Air Rescue, Seattle Division. Go ahead, *Boreas*."

Ross gave his name, paused and began reciting the latitude and longitude of the crash site.

"Hold on," the voice said. "Isn't this Commander Keough?"

119

"No," Ross said wearily. "I'm one of the meteorologists here. Is that good enough?"

"Sure. Now what were those coordinates again?" Ross heard faint shouting and the sounds of confusion on the other end, then, "Say, this is terrific. We've got the location plotted, and we'll send in a search and rescue plane as soon as the storm subsides."

"You can't wait that long," Ross replied. "You have to get those people out right away."

"I understand how you feel, Moran. But the fact is no plane exists that could land and take off safely in that wind. Another crash won't help matters one bit. No, we just have to wait it out."

Ross slapped the negative down on the control panel, a strong sense of resigned defeat welling up in him as the impact of the final statement from Earth penetrated. His effort would go for nothing; by the time the rescue plane could make its way to the shuttle the survivors would all be dead.

He plodded back to his room where sleep, so long denied, finally found him.

CHAPTER THIRTEEN

Briefly, Ross was a hero of sorts. It was a turn of events no one, least of all himself, would have predicted that following morning. It all began quite normally.

He was barely awake from what had been a distinctly unsatisfying sleep, had not washed or shaved yet, and was making his way to the station's galley for a much-needed dose of hot coffee. Vaguely he heard a shouted greeting and noticed a tall figure striding toward him down the length of the corridor in wide, swinging steps. It was Tim.

"I just heard all about it," he told Ross in exultation, "that was great work. Really great work."

Ross returned the only expression he could manage at that point: a blank stare of pure bafflement.

"Finding the shuttle, man!" said Tim, thumping Ross on the back enthusiastically. "Everybody's talking about it, saying you're a positive genius. Come on, I'll buy you a drink."

"Coffee?"

"Anything at all. Anything you desire."

There was a small reception committee awaiting him at one of the tables, the Colberts stood up and clapped as Ross stepped through the doorway. Ross looked baffled.

"Oh, come off that, Ross," Myra Colbert exclaimed.

"You're famous now, and you have to act the part. Hemming and hawing and being bashful just won't do."

"Just a minute. Hold on. Before the three of you start turning me into the Man Of The Hour, you'd better remember that all I did was take those photos. Why, it wasn't even my own film at all; somebody else—"

"Somebody else nothing, Ross. You found the crash, and that's the important thing. You went on looking after the rest of us gave up on those poor people."

Embarrassment was building up in him, but Myra's statement swept it away. Ross asked, startled, "People? You mean some actually did survive—they're . . . *alive?*"

He hardly dared to speak the final word.

"Seven out of fifty-nine lived through it," Joel Colbert explained. They were frostbitten and a livid blue-black, but definitely alive when the rescuers arrived at the coordinates Ross had passed to Air Rescue headquarters.

"I don't follow you," Ross protested, sipping at a proffered cup of steaming black coffee. "How could a plane get through the storm?"

"That's the best part," Tim said. "There was a way to reach the crash site that totally avoided contact with the storm. Since the shuttle went down on the Arctic Ocean ice sheet itself a Soviet submarine was able to travel beneath the stormy surface. With your data it broke through the ice about ten yards from the shuttle. You were exactly on target."

"That's the best thing I've heard so far," Ross replied, thoroughly happy.

"Finish that coffee quick. One of the news services wants to interview you as soon as you can stand up straight," Myra said excitedly, her voice ringing in the little room like an alarm bell.

The newsman was polished and persistent all through the interview. He insisted on dragging every possible minor detail out of Ross. A full hour of long-distance radio-telephoning was required before the reporter decided he had enough material for his article about the discovery and rescue of the shuttle crash victims.

When, at long last, the reporter terminated the call, Ross hung up the receiver with a sigh of relief that the whole absurd business was now finished. With any luck his part in the rescue would be forgotten quickly. And he could return to his work the same as before.

After all, he reasoned, what with the enormous events occurring on Earth—two great nations at the brink of open warfare—the average man would not be very curious about the exploits of a young meteorologist on a remote space station.

As it turned out, Ross was nearly correct.

The news services mentioned his name a few times in their write-ups, then promptly forgot about him. Whatever esteem the crew of *Boreas* had held him in faded rapidly with his blessings. His return to normality seemed to be proceeding at a fine clip, when he was told to report to Commander Keough's office.

Three hours had passed since the interview, and Ross wondered what she would have to say about it, if anything.

When he arrived, she did not take long coming to the point.

"Please sit down," she said. "I am given to understand you were responsible for locating the passenger shuttle crash?"

"Yes."

"Then you are to be congratulated for your skill. I am pleased that a member of this station's crew located the site after all. One item does not please me, however, and I think you know what it is."

Does she think I'm clairvoyant? Ross said to himself. If so, she's wrong, he thought, looking at that unruffled, enigmatic face. Her eyes were clear and unperturbed, her mouth tightly set, her hair perfectly arranged with no fine, steely strand out of place. She was calm, unhurried, and completely in control.

Ross was nervous. "I'm afraid I don't."

"Then let me refresh your memory, Mr. Moran. Before you started to search for the shuttle crash I asked that any and all findings should go to my office for transmission to the ground. You do recall that, don't you?"

Ross nodded and she continued. "Why, then, did you ignore my request? Why wasn't I informed you had discovered the crash site?"

"You were sleeping, I think."

"You think?" she said flatly.

"Well, as I remember your office was closed up. So was Mar—the assistant's. Nobody was about because it was very late by the time I'd finished processing the films. I had no other course but to call Earth myself."

"You don't consider that a trifle brash?"

"No," Ross said firmly.

"Even though you did not have the authorization?"

"I didn't know I needed authorization," replied Ross, now feeling a surge of anger creeping into his voice, "in an emergency."

That had some effect. She dropped her aloof expression like a discarded mask.

"That's hardly pertinent," she shot back. "The reason I asked that you inform me before any other agency—such as Air Rescue—is this: what if you were mistaken, your data incorrect? Have you considered the damage that might have ensued if you had been wrong?"

Ross had not, since the opposite had so obviously been the case.

Commander Keough regained her composure again automatically. The mask went back on.

"Permit me to inform you of what would have happened. Not on you would the blame be placed, but on myself for failing to exercise my position of command over this station. To put it plainly, I am responsible for the reliability of everything here. The crew, the machinery, and the data they gather. When you called Air Rescue without so much as a by your leave you placed me in jeopardy."

She gave Ross a stern look of warning and said, "This is the second time you have made an inexcusable error, the kind of error I can neither tolerate or forgive. I cannot allow this to continue, Mr. Moran. Should you miscalculate again I will be forced to dismiss you from the station."

"I understand, I guess," Ross mumbled apologetically. He had been expecting the threat since the conversation took its shape, but deep down he was far from cowed. He knew he had acted wisely when he decided to call Air Rescue on his own, rather than waiting for the proper "authority" to give him the nod. This wasn't a question of regulations, Ross came to realize, but a fundamental disagreement about a judgment made when the rules seemed dangerously at odds with the situation.

Despite Commander Keough's critical attitude, Ross took a measure of pride in his actions. For the first time in months he believed in his own worth. It was a strong conviction that he had done the right thing, and yet in a curious way Ross found himself agreeing with Commander Keough.

He had no desire at all to cross her again.

Their conversation, clearly, was at an end. Ross looked about for some excuse to break the thick silence and make a dignified and graceful retreat from her office. There was none. He rose from his seat, uncomfortably aware that her eyes were directed at him, appraising his awkwardness.

He paused by the doorway.

"Would you be interested in seeing the films? They're excellent quality."

"I don't believe so," answered Commander Keough, already becoming involved in a sheaf of papers on her desk.

Ross turned away and started to close the door when he heard her speak.

"Wait, Mr. Moran. There is something I would like to know. How did those films come into your possession?"

Ross explained. Commander Keough listened closely and took several notes as Ross spoke.

"And you say that this film was experimental, high-resolution, and yet this fellow—what was his name? —Dr. Ahn, *gave* it to you?"

"To pass along to Dr. Nystrom," Ross replied.

"I wonder if the U.S. Air Force knows its supplies are being distributed so liberally?"

Ross shrugged. "Since it was intended to be used in radio astronomical work, I suppose Dr. Ahn figured that Dr. Nystrom was the logical person to test it out."

"Yes, I imagine that you're correct. Thank you."

That was the first time in well over a day that Dr. Nystrom's name had come up, and before long Ross was calculating the number of hours remaining before he returned.

The radio astronomer had departed *Boreas* station a little over fifty hours before, so about twenty hours remained until he returned. He wondered if the space-wandering scientist had reached his goal and was now heading back toward his eventual rendezvous with the station.

Ross decided to search out the person who would know.

"Haven't heard a thing," Tim said.

"No transmission—at all?"

"It's not so unusual," Tim said. "He has his hands full running the tug and the radar and computing his orbit. Probably isn't getting half the shuteye he thought he would."

"Doesn't it bother you not receiving any word from him?" Ross said after a moment's consideration.

Tim shook his head. "If anybody else was piloting the tug I would have to answer, yes, of course. Dr. Nystrom's different. I think he knows more about flying a tug than any of those pilots you see down on Main Station who draw twice his salary. He knows what he's doing all the time and doesn't allow himself to get flustered."

Ross was forced to agree when Tim reminded him

126

of Dr. Nystrom's performance during the reactor accident. "He didn't get shook at all," Ross said.

Tim nodded. "He's like that always. Sane and healthy. The perfect patient, except he's so good he never *is* a patient." Tim smiled. "Dr. Nystrom's quite a character. The only one who measures up to him, actually, is our beloved station commander."

"I never thought I would hear you say that."

"Well," Tim replied a little sheepishly, "I am just trying to get my attitudes turned around concerning her. Try to change my opinion of her, you know, the way Dr. Nystrom suggested."

"Sounds as though you're having better luck than me," said Ross. "I just had a run-in with her about procedure. She took offense because I didn't alert her when the shuttle was located."

Tim slumped forward in his chair. They had been talking in the dispensary for several minutes, and Ross had been speculating that Tim was holding something back. He was right. The young doctor seemed to collapse.

"I was lying to you," he said despondently. "My attitude about Eva Keough hasn't changed; in fact I think it's about to get much worse. A while ago she ordered me to cease giving Julian Martino his daily antiradiation injection. Just like that! No explanation. According to her I'm to pack up his medicines along with some syringes and his medical records and deliver them to her office by six o'clock."

"How important are his drugs?" Ross said.

"Plenty. A person with a radiation burn like his doesn't recover in a month or two; the dosages have to be consistent for almost a year. If he's deprived of them he will die."

"I don't see why she would take such a step. Did she say Martino wasn't to receive any more injections at all?"

"Not exactly. Just that I'm not supposed to give them. Or have his drugs in the dispensary."

"Then he might be transferred to some place other

than *Boreas* in the near future," Ross suggested. "He could take his medicine with him, then, after you had it packed and ready for shipment."

"I'll concede that's possible," Tim replied. "In fact, that's what I thought immediately after she called the order to me. But then I had to stop and think, where in the wide world could Julian Martino be transferred where there's not an existing supply of his stuff. It's a standard provision on every ISA space station and vehicle, right alongside the painkillers and the eyewash in the medical chests on even the smallest ships. It doesn't add up, Ross. No matter how I look at it, there's a piece missing. And from what I can gather, it's no small item either."

CHAPTER FOURTEEN

Such was the rhythm and patter of his daily life that Ross sometimes forgot where he was. The very design of the station seemed to help foster the illusion that *Boreas* was not, in fact, in a long elliptical orbit around the Earth, but was instead anchored in terra firma. Ross found it easy to imagine that he was back in one of the enormous dormitory-classroom-laboratory complexes at his Pasadena, California *alma mater*.

He could recall having spent entire weeks inside one of those structures, eating, sleeping, studying for finals and even going to dances and movies without once venturing into the sunlight and the open air. It was a little weird and disconcerting when he stopped to think about it. Save for differences in gravity, there was a striking similarity between that time and the present; and he had completely adapted to the station's one-tenth gravity in the rotating section. The dreamy slowness of things falling, the wide springing strides he now took, the overall effortlessness of any motion he made was second nature, unnoticed, and unexciting. He had so accepted his new life on *Boreas* that something truly physically extraordinary was required to remind him that, indeed, he was a very long way from his own world.

It happened an hour after he had left the dispensary. Ross had been occupied cleaning the darkroom he

129

had used to process the infrared films earlier. He found the room in a state of confusion, trays of chemicals and racks lay everywhere in stagnant pools of water in the sink. The light table was sticky with old developing fluid. Various uncapped bottles and carboys were scattered about. He set about straightening the mess as best he could, swabbing down the table with a damp sponge and arranging the liquid containers in a semblance of order. When he turned on the tap he saw it.

The stream of water descended from the spigot in a thin transparent ribbon. Where on Earth the water striking the bottom of the sink would have merely burbled and fallen into the drain, the reduced gravity here produced a completely unexpected effect. It splattered high into the air, a white and intricate web of droplets like Queen Anne's lace, before slowly tumbling back to strike and burst upwards again.

Ross watched, totally fascinated, astonished that something as utterly commonplace as falling water could produce a beauty this captivating and pleasurable.

The water was cold to his touch as it splashed in the sink. Reluctantly, he turned his eyes from the wonder and started to dump the pans of chemicals he had used the previous night. One contained several of the negatives. Ross hadn't bothered to examine these three, and curiosity got the better of him. He held them up to the light. They were slimy and dripped on his shirt-front and Ross almost cast them into the waste can. Something he had seen on one of the films stopped him, and he spread them out on the light table for a closer inspection.

There was a dime-sized marking in the center of one negative. Ross had never seen anything like it before, and he bent over it with the most powerful magnifier in the darkroom.

The mark was a perfect circle. Around it was the storm, streaks of blue and yellow as in the other photos; however, not a wisp of color showed within the perimeters of the circular marking. Nothing but a hazy black outline. Ross scratched his sideburn, puzzled.

It was several minutes before he had an answer.

What he was seeing, he was sure now, was an object suspended above the storm. Probably it was a satellite, a large satellite; its proximity to the Arctic indicated it would have to be in a polar orbit. Only one satellite this large in such an orbital path existed, Ross was sure.

Inadvertently, Ross had photographed the *Basketball*. Which was most peculiar, Ross said to himself, since the infrared film appeared to reveal a dark shape inside the envelope or skin of the satellite.

Ross returned his gaze to the magnifier, hoping to make out more details. The marking was too blurred and indistinct.

Then the intercom rang. Three loud pulses.

Ross started nervously and switched on the speaker.

"This Ross?" came a faint whisper.

"Speaking," he replied. "Who is this?"

"Tim."

"How about speaking up a bit?"

"Can't." Still a whisper. "Are you awfully busy right now?"

"Hardly. What's the problem?"

There was no answer. The speaker clicked off at the other end.

Before a minute passed, Tim poked his head in, glanced about the room, and eased his way in and shut the door until the lock engaged.

He wore a worried expression on his face from the moment he entered.

"I think my intercom is being tapped," he said, still in a low voice. "And yours may be also."

"How do you know that?" Ross said.

"The moment I switched my speaker on, I could hear another person's breathing, followed by a buzzing noise. I think that was a tape recorder."

"Then why did you bother to whisper if it was being taken down?" said Ross.

"Natural reaction, I guess. Though it probably wasn't worth the effort."

Some of the skepticism must have showed in Ross's face, for Tim hastily added, "I know it sounds like I'm over the edge, Ross. But I swear it all happened the way I told you."

"The way life's been recently I suppose it is possible," Ross said.

"I'm glad to see you understand."

"I didn't say that, exactly," Ross said abruptly. "But it's no matter. What's on your mind?"

"The news finally came through, about the shuttle crash." Tim paused, his fingers trembling slightly where they gripped the edge of the sink. The color seemed to have drained out of Tim's face for that moment as he turned and looked directly at Ross.

"Jonathan Hanks is dead," he said tonelessly.

The darkroom reverberated Tim's words.

Ross's eyes widened in horror and shock.

"Yes, it is true. He was killed when the shuttle went down. The authorities just finished identifying the victims. His name was right there on the list. Just to make sure I checked with his employers on Main Station. They confirmed he was leaving via the passenger shuttle to Earth. To London. On January first."

"I—I just can't believe that," Ross said. A numbness was spreading through him.

"You must remember him talking about going back home to England," Tim said. "He said he would stay there until he'd accumulated enough evidence to compile a full report to the ISA."

Now the memory of the scene came flooding into Ross's mind: the cafe, the round tables with checkerboard cloths, the celebrating tourists, and the bright, happy conversation.

"This sort of shoots that idea to bits, doesn't it," said Ross a moment later. "Hanks had collected that information by himself, and he knew more than either of us about what's been going on. Did he keep any records of it, I wonder?"

Tim shook his head, saying, "He was smart enough not to have that kind of material in his possession. No, Hanks had a good memory for details; he stored away what he saw and read in the safest place, his head . . ."

"So that's the end of it, then, isn't it?" Ross said. "Hanks is gone, along with everything he picked up to use in that report. There's nothing to go on, now."

"It looks like that, I'll agree. Looks like we're back at the beginning again," Tim conceded reluctantly.

"A big pile of suspicions," said Ross ruefully, "but not a shred of evidence. That's what we've always needed, good, solid documented evidence on Martino and Commander Keough. Accusations require proof."

"Getting angry's not going to bring any in," Tim cautioned.

"I can't help it," said Ross in an agitated voice. "It really tears me up when I remember the two of them always feeding me that spiel about observing the regulations and respecting their authority. Hypocritical nonsense! Every single second they are aboard they violate the ISA charter, and nobody does anything about it!"

He stood there, his muscles aching with fury. Then, as quickly as it had crept into him, the rage left him.

Ross looked at his friend. "Now it's my turn to assure you I haven't fallen over the edge, either," said Ross in a quieter tone. "I guess you're right, we're back at the start. We have to begin all over, without any assistance."

"That's what I was hoping to hear you say," Tim said. "What information Hanks uncovered, we can also. I'm sure of it."

He got up and glanced at his watch. "Time for me to get a move on. I still haven't crated up Martino's medicine, and it's nearly six. I thought I could find a suitable carton over in central storage. What do you think"

"It's possible," Ross said. "I'll go with you. It's a large area to cover if you're pressed for time."

"Thanks, Ross, I could use the assistance."

"Don't mention it. Anything to help Julian Martino on his way.

Central storage was located not far from the darkroom.

"We're looking for a container the size of a lunchbox," Tim said. "Sing out if you spot one, OK?"

Ross set off down an aisle between stacks of electrical components and replacements for the station's standby system of fuel cells. Each carton was neatly labeled and sealed in clear plastic, so Ross tried the next aisle. He squeezed between two small mountains of paint canisters and emerged with considerable relief showing on his face. Moving down a third line, he thought he found a box the proper size, but when he tried to lift it, it turned out to be filled with unexpectedly heavy brass fittings.

Sprawling backwards, his shoulder brushed against a slick, cold surface. He gave it a cursory glance; it was one of three dusty oxygen cylinders, each half again as tall as he was and colored a vivid sea-green.

Ross rubbed his shoulder and began to walk away, recalling dimly his previous encounter with the great iron tanks. Something turned over in his brain, and he struggled to recollect the details of that night. Only the unmistakable hue of the cylinders persisted.

Ross swung around, frowning. Concentrating.

Yes, the tanks still had their wire caps intact, and though the dust lay a trifle thicker the warning tags were still quite legible.

He called hoarsely for Tim. A prickling fear broke in him as he stared ahead.

... *those tanks* ...

Tim arrived holding a small carton. "You didn't need to yell," he said, unconcerned. "I just found a box myself."

Ross ignored that and pointed to the cylinders. "Weren't those supposed to be installed in the tug before Dr. Nystrom took off?"

"Sure. I made a requisition when the tug's supply got that low," he said and tapped the side of one tank

134

with his knuckles. There was a low resounding boom. "These are the empties."

"Then why are they still sealed up and dusty from sitting in central storage for *months?*"

Tim craned his neck. "That is . . . strange," he said. "The maintenance crew must have substituted another set for these three. There's a master list of these kind of procedures; it's kept by the main docking collar, I think."

He was right. The list was clipped to the wall, conveniently located so persons debarking from the tug could indicate the need for supplies to be added. Tim pulled the checklist down and scanned the columns the moment they reached the docking area.

"According to this," he said, waving the list, "the tug's empty tanks were not replaced, not since two months ago. Not only that, but take a look at what happened to my requisition to have more oxygen loaded."

He handed Ross a sheet of paper. There, in Tim's usual lopsided script was the notation on a standard requisition form, plainly directing the installation of three tanks in the tug. It was quite unmistakable.

A heavy X mark crossed the order, and the words CANCEL REQUISITION had been added deliberately.

Ross realized what had occurred at that instant; Dr. Nystrom had flown the tug away, unaware that the amount of air remaining was already virtually exhausted. A simple calculation showed that this residue could last him only—at most—a dozen hours. By now over sixty had passed.

No wonder there had been no communications with the tug. Someone had made quite certain of that. It was a homicidal act of the simplest and most direct fashion; deprive a man of the air he must breathe and he dies.

That moment of realization lengthened imperceptibly; he felt locked by some strange inner paralysis that refused to release him even as a group of darkly

135

clad men broke into the room with shouts of "they're here!"

Immensely strong arms spun him around and shoved him roughly against the steel bulkhead and pinned him there. Ross felt his head jerked forward as his shoulders collided with the wall behind him. The taut muscles in the base of his neck snapped it backwards and his skull and the wall met with the sound of kindling crackling. . . .

The red mist in his eyes faded into the image of Commander Eva Keough's face. She was standing a few feet from him, before a half-dozen figures dressed as she was in form-fitting ebony coveralls, low boots, and narrow black belts with sidearm holsters.

Ross turned to look for Tim. The pain was incredible and he groaned slightly.

"Ah, you awaken," Eva Keough said. "Though it matters little, for you will be leaving soon. Leaving *Boreas* forever."

"What does that mean? You're going to destroy me, like Dr. Nystrom?" said Ross shakily.

"I doubt another tug could be spared. Come, come, Mr. Moran, I was joking."

"How can another person's death be humorous? I can't imagine the jury at your murder trial being so lighthearted."

Eva Keough smiled slightly and patiently explained, "There will be no trial, since Dr. Nystrom died as part of an ongoing military action. This action, which you see here, is another phase."

"I don't know what you're talking about. But I know that you work for the ISA, and the ISA will try you for his death," replied Ross.

"You have not been listening. I told you this is an action of the combined armed forces. My allegiance to the ISA has been severed. I resume my regular status as a military officer from this point on."

"Then you're breaking the treaty of Vienna!" Ross cried.

"The treaty is a dead letter," Eva Keough said coolly.

"I'll bet the ISA doesn't think so."

"The ISA is helpless. If it were not so, all this would be unnecessary. You can be assured that I have no desire to transship both you and Mr. Diehle to a place of safety. I would as soon leave you here and let life go on as before."

"I'm going nowhere at all," Ross shot back angrily. "I have rights as a citizen."

She shook her head. "You have no rights. This is a matter of national—" she caught herself and carefully corrected her sentence. "Of world security, and as such you are under martial law."

"I don't believe it. Where is Tim?"

"Colonel Martino is questioning him at present. You needn't worry about him."

"I'm worrying. What have you got against Tim?"

"He is under suspicion," said Eva Keough, "of consorting with the enemy. And, I might also add, so are you."

"*That* is the most fantastic thing I have ever heard a human being say."

She said nothing for a moment.

"You will admit that you were a close acquaintance of Dr. Nystrom?" she asked him.

"Of course. Before you killed him."

Her voice was loaded with exasperation. "Your 'close acquaintance' was one of a ring of agents that has infiltrated the higher levels of government and science, especially the ISA. Until Military Intelligence became aware of their presence, these agents operated freely both on Earth and here—in space. They have been among us for many years, completely unsuspected, waiting and working towards a strike at the centers of world government with some new variety of long-range weapon."

"You actually believe Dr. Nystrom is involved in that?"

"Another of your 'acquaintances,' the one you knew as Jonathan Hanks, admitted as much."

137

"Hanks!" Ross said in astonishment. "Hanks died in the shuttle crash."

"Yes, he died from his injuries. But not before the security officer of the Russian submarine *Sannikov* questioned him."

"Impossible," Ross said firmly. "He wasn't a spy, and neither was Dr. Nystrom. And Tim isn't one, either."

"Do not be so eager to defend him," Eva Keough said. "For Military Intelligence has in its possession a letter Hanks sent Mr. Diehle. It is a very incriminating document and establishes a link between them that would be difficult to refute."

Ross's heart sank. The letter! So they all knew about it, after all. But how had it become twisted around into this brand of insanity?

"Hanks told the Soviet security officer many other items. For instance, he revealed that Dr. Nystrom's friend, the Korean astronomer Dr. Ahn, is another member of the ring. He has just been captured and is now being interrogated in Denver. The only thing he has revealed thus far is something we have known for some time—that a weapon exists, hidden beyond the Earth's surface, in space. In a few more hours he will reveal its location."

"Then," she said with a note of expectant triumph in her voice, "we will deal with it."

Her eyes gleamed.

Ross heard a door open nearby and a bitter exchange of voices, and then Tim was being herded into the room by Julian Martino. Colonel Julian Martino. He stood Tim up beside Ross, then moved back and drew his automatic. He leveled it at Tim and swung the muzzle to face Ross.

To Ross's eyes, Tim appeared somewhat groggy, and he guessed the young doctor had had some drug forced on him to help loosen his tongue. Tim swayed unsteadily and blinked in the light.

"Settle down, there!" Martino demanded loudly, swinging the gun back to point at Tim.

"Did he tell you anything important?" she said to Martino.

"Nothing." Martino scowled. "He knew only that we were still officers while in the ISA."

"That is all?" she said insistently. "What about the letter? And Hanks?"

"Nothing there, either. He was indulging his fantasies of being a detective," said Martino. "The serum should be wearing off shortly."

Tim shook his head. Alarmed, Martino centered the automatic on him and put a tense finger on the curved metal trigger.

"You are surprisingly jumpy," Eva Keough told him. "Here, let me take that thing before you attempt to use it on them." She took the heavy gun from her companion and held it loosely by her side.

Ross watched the exchange with more than polite interest. For he could see that though Martino had no skill with the gun, Eva Keough had even less. She held it awkwardly, as if it were something else entirely, a sliderule, perhaps, or a cup of coffee.

Ross felt a jolt transmitted through the metal bulkhead to his shoulder blades and simultaneously heard a scraping thump at the docking collar.

"Our transportation has arrived," Martino said with a look of satisfaction on his face.

"Exactly on schedule." Eva Keough looked at Ross. "Now comes the time when you will be removed to a safer place. I still have a few questions to put to you."

Ross glanced at Tim, who winked back. He was recovered. Praise be, Ross said silently. I sure don't want to go off with these maniacs by myself.

"Please stand by the entranceway," Eva Keough said smoothly. "And be ready to step inside when it opens—"

It was that tone of voice that did it, that cool and condescending quality that had irritated him in teachers and policemen and bureaucrats all his life. Right there, Ross decided he was not stepping blindly into their carefully prepared prison.

"No!" he screamed. "No, No, NO!"

Startled, Eva Keough lifted the automatic to aim for his face. She fumbled with the massive automatic for an instant, bringing her middle finger around the trigger to squeeze it and fire. There was no explosion, no metal slug driving through his skull into his cerebrum.

Instead of the solid crash he expected, there was a faint *click*.

Everything stood perfectly still. Ross suddenly realized that Eva Keough had not, in fact, just shot him dead. Her inexperienced fingers had snapped the safety catch on; the gun could not fire.

He turned to let Tim know, but the doctor had already grasped the essentials of the situation and was launching himself forward at Eva Keough.

She tugged vainly at the immovable trigger.

Tim connected.

The blow sent her sprawling into Martino, and the three of them piled into a steel scaffolding. Ross heard bones go snap. The automatic went pinwheeling through the air.

Tim was still moving. He batted the gun away from Martino's outstretched hand, flung him aside, and charged into the row of grim-faced men in black standing to one side. His wide shoulders carried them like a halfback.

Ross saw one of them going for his holstered weapon and started at him. Tim lunged for the man's waist and got there first, bowling them both over. He landed a left hook and the man went limp. Tim looked up at Ross and shook his head at a wide-open door a few yards distant.

"Go," Tim bellowed.

Ross paused, assessing the situation again; Tim was outnumbered something like seven to one. Bad odds. And if he went to aid his friend they wouldn't improve greatly, in the end, the guns would prevail.

"*Go on!*" Tim urged in a panting voice. "Get going." He meant it.

Ross turned and flung himself through the door. He

pulled it shut and dropped down the ladder into a deserted corridor. He started to run. Behind him and above, the door crashed open.

Ross could hear somebody shouting wildly, followed by a screech of dismay. Three gunshots echoed like rolls of high mountain thunder down the corridor as a black-clad figure opened up on him.

Ross ducked into a side corridor as the bullets slashed the wallboards.

There was a distant shot.

Then silence.

Another stream of bullets roared into the corridor. Ross swerved around a corner, leaped to another ladder, and descended it as quickly as he could make his arms and legs function.

A man appeared behind him and fired twice, and Ross could feel the first stirrings of panic race in his brain. He knew he had to get away. But where? The corridors were all alike, and suddenly unfamiliar. He felt lost. A horrible sense of dread settled over him now as he realized to the core of his being that his life was in enormous danger, and he had absolutely no idea how to see his way clear.

He got up and started running again, mindlessly. His eyes told him nothing except that he was moving, moving, moving. His lungs seemed to be burning, his heart slamming around like a machine. And the only thing that seemed coherent was the helpless thought that kept rising to his consciousness: Sammy, Sammy, was it this way in your last moments, too?

CHAPTER FIFTEEN

He leaned against the door frame inside his room. His knees were sagging and threatened to give way any minute if he did not rest awhile. His chest also sent him flashing warning arrows of pain each time he drew air into his lungs.

Ross allowed himself to slide to a sitting position and cocked his head toward the door, listening to the confusion of running feet in the corridors beyond.

Ducking, twisting, dodging his pursuers, Ross had been avoiding the black-clad men for what seemed like an eternity, but which he knew must be only a few minutes. His only thought at first was the primal urge to escape. Fortunately, *Boreas,* with its complexity of hallways and passages and separate levels, was a three-dimensional labyrinth in which a fleeing quarry could hide with some assurance of not being found.

When Ross realized that they had momentarily lost his trail, he controlled his panic and systematically went through his memory for a more suitable refuge. Of all places, his room seemed the most likely, it was small, with a lockable door and a basin with running water— all valuable considerations if he was forced into a lengthy seclusion.

And now he had made it. Quickly, Ross activated the door's pressure-sealing system, set the lock, and looked around.

142

The place was barely recognizable.

His bunk was rumpled and the mattress was slit in several spots. Bits of spongy stuffing material littered the floor in heaps. The contents of every one of his desk drawers was strewn everywhere. Someone had made a hasty—but thorough—search. Nothing seemed to be missing, however. Just relocated.

He rose from the metal deck and stretched out wearily on the bunk. One of the metal bedsprings poked through the mattress, jabbing into his shoulder blade. The sharp stinging almost made him cry out, but it also drove the haziness from his eyes and cleared his mind. He was alert again.

All was quiet, except the slight purr of air from the vent. No voices, now. No shouting or footsteps.

It could mean one of two things. Either they had given up their search for him, or were regrouping to make a methodical room-by-room examination of *Boreas* until he was discovered. Ross could not believe Eva Keough had called off her men already. No, it was much more probable that they were going to tear the station apart, if necessary, looking for him.

Ross refused to consider the consequences of capture. He hunched down, planning his next move. A place to hide, obviously. But where? His little compartment appeared to offer little in the way of concealment, being little more than a rectangular space with a few pieces of utilitarian furniture set about at random.

Not too promising. The possibilities of his finding a decent refuge seemed limited to two. He could pry off the vent grille and squeeze in there, probably, and replace the grille after he was set. Then there was his bunk. He knew that there was a crawlspace about two feet deep between the bedsprings frame and the deck itself; it would be enough to ensconce himself when the time came, as he knew it would.

Nothing to do now, he told himself, except wait for the inevitable. Soon as I hear doors opening and closing down the hallway I burrow in and hang tight.

"Ross Moran!" the hallway speaker blared.

143

"Ross Moran," Eva Keough's voice repeated at twenty times her natural volume, "you have three minutes to report to the docking area and surrender. I am making preparations to depart, and I fully intend to shut down the station completely. Electrical power will be cut and all oxygen vented into space. You now have two minutes and forty-five seconds remaining!"

Ross weighed the terms of Eva Keough's warning. The loss of electricity would be of minimal importance, the lighting would go out along with the water circulation pumps and some other related systems. And the motors that rotated the station to produce the artificial gravity he was experiencing at this moment would stop, too.

Even a return to complete lack of gravity paled before the threat of *Boreas* stripped of its interior atmosphere. All Ross had to do was recall Dr. Nystrom's end to bring him to serious consideration of surrender.

He didn't make a move to do so. He couldn't, knowing that Tim had deliberately provided Ross with the means of escape; to capitulate now would be nothing less than betrayal.

"Two minutes. I am shutting down the reactor. Give up."

The overhead illumination panels were flickering. Ross estimated he had about another minute of light remaining, so he frantically set to work combing through the debris in his room. Just as the speaker shattered the silence again, his fingers closed around the familiar flat aluminum casing of Sammy's flashlight. Simply holding it in his hand was a tie to the past and a comforting reassurance that he was not dependent on the resources of *Boreas* station.

"One minute remaining now, Mr. Moran," the speaker roared. Eva Keough's normally calm and detached tone of voice held a streak of annoyance.

"You must surrender immediately. Do not be foolish, Mr. Moran. Do not waste your life this way."

That was all she said. Shortly afterward, the filaments in the ceiling panels ceased glowing altogether.

Ross switched on the flashlight to low beam. Sitting there on the bed, he hardly needed the illumination. It was more an act of defiance.

What alarmed him was the gradual fading away of the air flow from his vent. As the pumps halted it dropped to a trickle and then to nothing at all.

Abruptly there was an ominous sound.

Suction.

Air was being withdrawn from his room.

At first it was nearly inaudible like a slow leak. But rapidly it turned into a frightening *whoosh*. Ross jumped up and slammed the vent grille shut.

Out in the corridor he heard a high keening gale howling as the station's air supply spilled out into space. Then the station started to react as the air pressure dropped towards zero, automatically a series of metal barriers fell into place, dividing *Boreas* into self-contained segments. Bolts rammed home and heavy locking bars rumbled into their niches. The station was secure, now, Ross thought, as he heard a final faraway thud.

Eva Keough and her crew had left the station. From this moment forward he was alone, trapped in this tiny cellful of oxygen. Ross could tell that his supply would not last for long; already it had acquired an unmistakable flatness, and each breath drawn seemed less and less satisfactory.

It was time to move. At the end of the corridor was an emergency oxygen system. Ross figured that was Target Number One. Once he had secured a portable breather, he felt he could begin to plot a wider course of action with a reasonable chance of success. But first it would have to be that breather unit.

He thumbed the flashlight to high and pushed his door open. He whirled out into the corridor, propelled by the room air gusting forth, and ran for the breather unit which lay sealed in a plastic blister. Ripping through the transparent bubble, Ross grabbed the breather and activated the mask section, luxuriating in the cold dry smell of the oxygen flow.

He unclipped the bottle and strapped it to his back. In the flashlight beam he could see this section of corridor was blocked at both ends by steel slabs that would not yield to his probing fingers. They were dogged down rigidly with no hope of moving until the atmosphere was brought back to normal pressure.

Ross returned to his room, gloomily aware now that he had escaped from this prison cubicle into nothing more than a larger cell block.

One route alone could lead him out of this subdivided maze.

The vents. They honeycombed *Boreas,* connecting every compartment and living area. Narrow and constricting though they were, the vents offered the only means of movement inside the station and Ross knew he had to accept it.

Standing on his bunk, he wrenched off the grille slats, exposing a hexagonal opening the width of his shoulders. He barely fit; the combined bulk of his body and the breather tank plugged the aperture at first. Ross unstrapped the oxygen bottle and shoved it ahead of him. Inch by inch he crawled down the tunnel. The flashlight beam reflected weirdly on the polished metal sides.

A much wider and taller tube intersected several yards further. Ross followed it eagerly for a distance, then his oxygen bottle struck a steel mesh that had been stretched across the tunnel, completely obstructing the way ahead.

He thought first of backing up, and quickly rejected the idea, there was not space enough in the tube to turn around and Ross felt no desire to go where his eyes could not appraise him of the route. He might back into a pump, he thought, or a turbine blade.

No, the mesh had to be removed, and soon, too, since the gauge on the breather registered a little more than four minutes of air remaining. The mesh was welded in position firmly. His hands could detect no weak point. Damn! Ross sat back, thinking furiously that he would have to butt the mesh open using the

146

oxygen bottle. It was a delicately risky maneuver, since the air inside was under high pressure. Ross had heard stories of skindivers who accidentally let their oxygen tanks fall. The effect was generally compared to a stick of TNT detonating.

The meter dropped to three minutes.

Ross shrugged. He gripped the cylinder with both hands, instinctively shut his eyes and rammed the bottle against the mesh as hard as he could.

The mesh clattered away.

He pushed on past it for a few feet until he discovered a grille set in the side of the tunnel. Ross batted it with the oxygen cylinder and managed to dislodge it.

He stepped out into the pantry. Trays of frozen food carpeted the deck. The coffeemaker had burst open. It was chaos. Ross picked his way to the door, through the kitchen and dining area, and passed on down the hallway where another breather was located.

Not long afterwards Ross ascended the ladder that led to the docking area. He glanced around for signs of Eva Keough's departure and saw only a few scraps of black cloth and a single smear of dried blood on the deck.

Nearby was the auxiliary control room. In this place Eva Keough had shut down the nuclear generator and dumped the station's atmosphere. In half an hour Ross had sufficiently familiarized himself with the banks of circuitry to reverse the process.

The illuminating panels returned to life first, then the dump valves closed and air circulators started pouring fresh oxygen into *Boreas* station. When Ross heard the sectional barriers begin to roll back all over the station he pulled the breather from his face.

He inhaled and stretched. It was glorious.

All around him the station hummed like a large, contented animal. Ross turned away from the controls and was leaving the room when he imagined he saw through an observation port the rotation navigation beacon at the nose of a spacecraft looming against the curtain of stars. It must have been a blinking light on the control panel reflecting on the thick glass, Ross told himself. The explanation was logical, but it also was wrong.

Ross heard the characteristic scraping of two metallic surfaces meeting, and then the whine of the docking collar locks engaging and gripping the hull of a familiar stubby vehicle. After sixty-nine hours, the long-gone tug had returned.

Dr. Alfred Nystrom stood in the auxiliary control room, removing his heavy gloves and allowing them to float beside him while he examined one of Ross's infrared negatives.

"You know," he said, "if this marking is the *Basketball,* and I suspect it is, and there is some kind of large mechanism concealed inside, then everything ties together."

"There's one rather large *if* you can't still account for," Ross said after a moment's thought. "You can't be positive the device *is* a laser, as you suggested."

Dr. Nystrom attempted to scratch his elbow, a difficult undertaking since he had not yet shed his thick spacesuit.

"I ran the results through the tug's computer several times; the results always agreed. The *Basketball* and the relay satellite were within ten miles of one another when the relay ceased to transmit. Obviously the men on the *Basketball* became jittery when the relay swung near—"

"—and opened fire," said Ross, completing the thought.

"No other explanation accounts for the relay's condition. When I recovered it, it was fused into an unrecognizable lump of metal slag," Dr. Nystrom said.

Ross found it hard to disagree. He was still recovering from the shock of Dr. Nystrom's reappearance, and more than once he found himself wondering if, indeed, he was talking to some lively phantom. But phantom

148

or not, Dr. Nystrom had a point that Ross could not refute.

The spacecraft Eva Keough and her people had boarded from *Boreas* station was headed for the *Basketball*. Dr. Nystrom had tracked her departure orbit with the tug's radars from the moment she cast off after cutting the power to the automatic docking system on *Boreas*. The thing that bothered Ross was Dr. Nystrom's next tactic. He intended to follow her there.

"You'll be placing yourself in exactly the position she wants," Ross protested. "She admitted that she ordered your tug to leave without enough oxygen. If she has a laser, she'll be sure to turn it on you, the same as the relay."

"That's exactly it, if the thing's a laser. It might not be, remember. I want to find out," he said flatly. "The tug has more than enough fuel for the maneuver, and I have the element of surprise."

"That's true. She still thinks you're the late Dr. Nystrom."

"Yes," he smiled at the thought. "I anticipate she will find it startling that I turned up in this good a condition!"

"I'm rather familiar with that sort of reaction," Ross said, "and it shall be interesting to see how close hers is."

It took a moment for the intent of his words to strike Dr. Nystrom.

"Wait, Ross! Nobody said you were coming along." He looked at Ross, and said, "You are serious, aren't you?"

Ross nodded. He had come to that decision and would not turn away from it now. Not for anything.

"You realize that everything you told me could apply to you as well. A laser will not discriminate."

"I have had my share of gunfire recently," Ross replied. "It doesn't discourage me half as much as the thought of staying here."

At last Dr. Nystrom acceded, and Ross started for the docking collar. Dr. Nystrom called him back.

149

"The tug's going nowhere until we have refilled all the oxygen tanks aboard."

"As far as I know the three green cylinders are still in central storage," Ross replied.

"That's not all of them. If it were so, I'd be a lot less healthy right now. The only thing that kept me alive was the fact that Eva Keough forgot there are five spacesuits kept in the tug; each has twelve hours of oxygen in the backpack tanks. They're all empty, and they're going to be refilled before we leave, also. Eva Keough can make her own errors," Dr. Nystrom said with a grim smile. "I don't intend to follow her example."

CHAPTER SIXTEEN

The final stage of the approach was under way.

Ross lowered the binoculars from his eyes with a sense of mingled disappointment and relief.

"No sign of the *Basketball* yet," he reported to Dr. Nystrom.

"I expected as much," he replied. "Until it moves into the sunlight it will remain pretty much invisible."

Both the tug and its target were orbiting a thousand miles over the night side of Earth now; momentarily their common course would bring them into the first rays of dawn. As the time drained away, Ross wiped the eyepiece and stared out through the canopy past the noise of the tug into the empty sky.

Execpt for the distant stars and the plump white half-moon off to one side, all was drowned in darkness: the planet below, the tug, and the *Basketball*. Ross found intensely unnerving the thought that the *Basketball* was in the immediate vicinity of the tug now and still it was undetected. Why, it might be sitting only a few yards away at this second, with its laser already warmed up and aimed at them. For the hundredth time, Ross wished he could persuade Dr. Nystrom to turn on the tug's radar and locate their quarry once and for all. And for the hundredth time Ross suppressed that anxious yearning.

For five hours, since they had departed *Boreas* station, Dr. Nystrom had been preparing for the upcoming confrontation. All during the long unpowered descent from the weather station to the low-altitude orbit of the Basketball, he calculated and revised the trajectory that would lead the tug to rendezvous with an eye towards a safe and undetectable approach. He decided to edge up to the *Basketball* as cautiously as possible; that meant all lights doused, radio and radars off.

Ross appreciated Dr. Nystrom's concern, but he wondered if he wasn't carrying caution a bit too far. After all, the assignment of determining the position of the *Basketball* had fallen to Ross, and he hadn't the faintest idea which section of the sky he should be scanning. His target could be anywhere in the inky depths. Ross figured it was a hit-or-miss proposition; finding the *Basketball* would be strictly a matter of luck, despite Dr. Nystrom's assurances that when the time arrived Ross would spot it easily.

Over the eastern edge of the planetary curve a slit of white light appeared first, followed by a section of yellow-white disk that rapidly climbed over the thin film of the Earth's atmosphere.

"Sunrise," Dr. Nystrom said triumphantly. "Stop worrying those binoculars, Ross. Look below and left of forward!"

Ross swung his head around. Dr. Nystrom was right, there was a flashing bubble of metal there. He set the binoculars on high power and peered down.

It was the *Basketball*. He estimated the gap between them was a little more than fifteen miles. A burst from the thrusters narrowed it to seven.

Ross groaned as the tug lurched forward in space, watching the point of light that was the *Basketball* expand into a shiny coin, and then bulge into a globe the size of an orange held at arm's length. The thrusters quit and the tug was silent once more, drifting slowly toward the glistening sphere.

The sun continued to rise over the Earth, spreading its light on the continents and ocean below.

They were crossing the South Pacific in a line almost

due south. The sea below was hard blue and streaked with gray cloud masses; to his right was the broad brown arch of the Australian coastline bordered by the thin broken line of the Great Barrier Reef standing seaward north and west. Ross strained in his seat straps and could barely make out a portion of the lonely coast of Tasmania. All else was obscured by a wide frontal system of dirty white cumulus to the horizon.

Ross heard a *click* in the cabin and turned swiftly around. Dr. Nystrom had switched on the radio receiver and was pointing the antenna at the *Basketball*.

"Seems to be commotion of some kind," he said after a minute with an earphone pressed to his head.

"Have we been spotted?" Ross said hesitantly. He swiveled to look at the *Basketball* again.

No alterations had taken place. It remained a vast round patchwork of aluminum sheets. The metallic sheen gave Ross the impression that the *Basketball* was solid through, like an enormous ball bearing, and he had to remind himself that in actuality it greatly resembled its namesake. It was no more than a large inflated envelope with a skin no more thick than his thumbnail.

"I don't think they've seen us. There's a lot of telemetry from and to Earth, and some coded messages, but no indication that they know we're here."

I don't understand how they could miss our presence, Ross thought. Seven miles apart. Practically docked!

"Wait a minute," Dr. Nystrom said, his voice becoming more agitated. "I'm picking up more traffic now. Code, telemetry, voice—the whole works. Hold on! Somebody just gave somebody else the go-ahead. There's a confirmation."

"What does that mean?"

"I have no conception," he said in reply. "Are you scared?"

"I don't know," Ross said. "Remembering what you told me about the relay, I guess I might be."

"I'll agree to that," Dr. Nystrom said soberly.

153

"There's no point to hanging around here any longer. I have no particular desire to see what happens next."

His trembling hand reached for the controls for the forward-firing thrusters. He never made it.

The *Basketball* exploded.

The aluminum surface rippled and stretched, then tore apart in a single soundless burst of gas and twisting fabric. Great strips of metal foil went whirling away from the center of the blast like leaves in a thunderstorm.

The gas that had so long kept the *Basketball* a rigid sphere dispersed in a moment in a wraithlike band of translucent crystals.

Faintly shrouded by the last wisps of gas, even now freezing into an icy dust, was some tremendous metal construction. As the final particles of gas thinned to nothingness, it floated like a new species of insect, revealed in the new day's harsh light.

Ross clung to his seat, keeping his eyes fixed on the glittering machine that lay in the distance. One end was roughly cylindrical and studded with a network of fins, while the other was a mass of convoluted dish antennae, probes and radars and transparent blisters—like a spider's head enlarged hundreds of times.

It turned slowly in space, exercising its booms and struts and pointing its antennae experimentally. For one nightmarish moment it aimed one directly at the tug, and Ross anticipated a searing laser blast to follow immediately. It did not.

The machine seemed disinterested, seemingly regarding the tug as one with the exploded debris that once had been the *Basketball*. It pivoted its antenna system flush to its hull, rotated northward.

A beam as bright as the surface of the sun erupted from the rear of the machine, and began moving instantly away. So rapid was its departure that Ross could keep it in sight for less than a heartbeat before it dwindled to a fading dot of light.

"What a fine spaceship," said Dr. Nystrom, his voice filled with admiration.

154

"So that's what killed the relay," Ross said.

Dr. Nystrom nodded in awe. "I've never seen anything like it. Must be the first one built. Constructed here, right under our collective noses, right inside the *Basketball.*"

Dr. Nystrom picked up the earphone assembly and was about to switch it off. A stray noise caught his attention and he held it up to his ear with an intent look.

"That's unusual," he said. "A very small radio is operating close by. A spacesuit transmitter, I guess."

The tug's tracking system located the faint signal and determined its position. "Just six miles. I'm going to have a look," Dr. Nystrom concluded, and, after Ross nodded his approval the tug started forward, gliding slowly through the drifted fog of gas and slivers of metal foil that hung near the ripped and deflated corpse of the *Basketball.* An object hove into view.

"It's a spacesuit, all right," said Ross. "The spaceship left somebody behind."

Inside the suit the figure was moving feebly, oblivious of the approach of the tug.

Dr. Nystrom opened the main cargo hatch. Using judicious bursts on the tiny verniers together with his considerable skill, he maneuvered the tug into such a position that momentum carried the person inside. He closed the hatch and pressurized the entire section.

Ross scrambled aft to the spacesuited figure. He saw that the faceplate was entirely misted over, and, alarmed, he removed the bulky helmet.

"Oh, my God," he yelled to Dr. Nystrom when the thing was finally unlatched. "It's Tim!"

Tim opened one rheumy eye. "Pipe down, there. I'm perfectly well," he said, breathing with difficulty.

"No, you're a rotten liar," Ross replied, unzipping the cumbersome spacesuit. What emerged from it made him stop, shocked. Tim was thoroughly battered, with reddish-purple welts on his shoulders and face, bruises on his neck, and a bullet wound in his upper right arm, crusted with brown drying blood.

155

"You really caught it," Ross said, shaking his head angrily.

"Comes from not talking," Tim said. "I didn't know what they wanted, and after I got drilled back on *Boreas* I was in no mood to cooperate."

He lifted his head a little. "That you, Dr. Nystrom?"

"The same," came the reply as Dr. Nystrom entered the compartment. "The hospital section on Main Station has just been alerted that you're heading there very soon."

"That's a depressing thought."

Ross brought over the first-aid kit and started dabbing some anesthetic on the wound. Tim smiled wanly and sat back. "My colleagues will never believe that I let a meteorologist perform anesthesia," he said. "There goes the profession."

"Rather do it yourself?" Ross said.

"No, I'm rather enjoying this sudden reversal in roles. Speaking of which," Tim said, jerking his head to one side to see Dr. Nystrom, "Eva Keough thinks you're a spy. Are you?"

"What do you think, Tim?"

"I knew you weren't," Tim said, and relaxed. "But what ever gave Military Intelligence the notion?"

"Probably the same logic that mixed you up in this."

"All of them are over the edge," Tim declared. "They hauled me off *Boreas* to the *Basketball* and pestered me with one question. Just one. They seemed to imagine that this fantastic ring of secret agents have a secret base somewhere. They actually believe something like that exists."

"Eva Keough mentioned that to me, too," Ross said. "I wonder what you told them."

"Easy with that bandage, Ross," Tim said in a professional tone of voice. "I said the thing was in Oz, or someplace equally mythical. Martino didn't know how to react. I think he was thrown for a while, but he realized fairly quickly, and I was afraid I might meet up with another .45."

Ross set the adhesive tabs on the bandage, securing it to the skin with a slight pressure. He moved back and judged his handiwork.

"It's a lucky thing you didn't," Ross said dispiritedly. "You'd be stuck with another one of my attempts at medicine."

"It'll do admirably, thank you." Tim paused, then said, "About that time Eva came bustling in, telling everyone to leave me be. She announced that your friend, Dr. Ahn, finally caved in after he had had enough truth serum pumped into him."

"Ross told me Dr. Ahn had been picked up," said Dr. Nystrom.

"I think Dr. Ahn is still being held in custody," Tim said, continuing. "What he said certainly stirred up Eva. She had taken command of the spaceship, and so she decided to take off and demolish this secret base she thinks exists. I was suited up and pitched out the airlock. The next thing I knew the spaceship was gone, and you two had shown up. Small universe."

"What did Dr. Ahn say, specifically?" Dr. Nystrom said.

"He must have been all muddled by the drugs. He said the base was on *Boreas*. Eva Keough's even more muddled, for she believes that's the location.

Dr. Nystrom said quickly, "You're sure that is their destination? *Boreas* station?"

"Our old home," Tim replied. "Won't be much left of it after she gets through with it, though."

"What do you mean?"

"That ship's well armed."

Dr. Nystrom took Ross aside and said in a whisper that the tug was set on automatic guidance. "The computer will fly both of you to Main Station within the hour," he said, moving toward the airlock hatchway.

"Both of us?" Ross said. "You're not going, too?"

"Not now. I have to return to *Boreas* immediately."

"You can't be serious. Eva Keough will blast it apart."

157

"Then, logically, I must stop her from doing so."

He was determined, Ross could see, and that forced an agonizing decision upon him. As much as he disliked the idea of sending Tim off by himself in the tug, Ross could not bear to think of deserting Dr. Nystrom now. When he told Tim he was gratified to see his friend quickly agree.

"Don't give it a second thought," Tim insisted. "I can take care of myself. Go on and make sure Dr. Nystrom doesn't get carried away trying to slow down Eva Keough."

Ross found a suit that fitted and struggled into the outfit. He and Dr. Nystrom entered the airlock and shut the inner hatch.

A moment later the outer door rolled back. Ross pushed himself into the star-filled sky, far away from the tug. In a minute the tug fired its engines and began its short tangential swing toward Main Station. Ross turned his eyes from the sight. Where was Dr. Nystrom? he wondered. And where was the vehicle they were supposed to be flying to *Boreas?*

Aside from a few crumpled scraps of foil, space was empty.

Ross twisted awkwardly, looking with a growing desperation for the spacesuited figure or the bright outline of another tug parked nearby. There was nothing.

Ross switched on the suit radio and called out.

No reply.

He was alone, drifting. A thousand miles under him was the Earth. Azure and emerald planet, it was lovely beyond description as the sunlight poured on its lands and waters. The half-moon still rode in solitude in the velvet deeps.

Ross jammed his eyes shut. He felt nothing but a strange dryness in the back of his throat.

Abruptly his hair stood on end over his entire body, and his skin seemed to be afire. A twinge of pain shot through him.

An enormous electrical tension was building.

The power cells in my suit are shorting out, Ross thought. In the next instant they will electrocute me. What a ridiculous way to die.

The sky split open and took him . . .

CHAPTER SEVENTEEN

. . . and set him down. Gently. With no more than a brittle snapping of the tension that had peaked inside him, Ross saw that he had *moved*.

He was floating just above a jumbled tangle of lines and angles and glistening surfaces. Multicolored lights flashed into existence. Then every discordant element came together in his consciousness, and he recognized his immediate surroundings with a tingling shock.

It was the radio astronomy lab on *Boreas* station.

Along the walls were the hunched consoles of the computer and the radio amplifiers. At the opposite end of the room was Dr. Nystrom, his hand resting on a lighted panel set in a wall cavity. He was gesturing with the other hand.

Ross released the bindings and took off his helmet. He was vaguely aware that Dr. Nystrom was speaking to him rapidly, asking a barrage of questions to which Ross could not begin to reply; his mind was posing more questions of its own than he could handle.

Primarily: *how* could he be here? And conversely, how could he be *here*? Or was he here at all? Was this scene a very vivid and convincing illusion dredged up from the depths of his memory? Or a detailed hallucination brought on by electrocution?

But he knew this wasn't a hallucination, or an illusion, or anything else. The lab was stable and solid before his eyes. It was real. There were no distortions evident but one.

Ross had traveled some thirty-five thousand miles between one heartbeat and the next. Somehow, he was on *Boreas* station.

Dr. Nystrom halted in midsentence. "You haven't heard one word I've said, have you?" he asked, nearly turning it into a statement of fact.

Ross nodded, looked about him, then at Dr. Nystrom.

"So what does it matter?" he said heavily. "You've succeeded in duping me this far. Why stop?"

Dr. Nystrom said nothing.

"Eva Keough was correct," Ross continued, seething with anger and self-contempt whipped together. "All along you were a spy."

The accusation burst Dr. Nystrom's calm demeanor. "You know that is complete nonsense. Eva Keough is not correct—she is totally mistaken, misled by her superiors, by her compatriots, and by her own fears of what she cannot understand."

"Do you seriously expect me to believe that?" Ross said bitterly.

"Don't let yourself be carried away, Ross, by her reactions of alarm and panic."

"She has good cause, it seems to me," Ross replied, indicating the wall-cavity control panel with a wave of his gloved hand. "It's all coming true, right in this room. Those controls have never been there before. That wall space has been a blank each time I've been in this place. What's been hiding there? Isn't it the weapon she was describing?"

"Well, no," Dr. Nystrom said. "You and she happen to be wrong. That controls a transportation system, no matter what delusions Military Intelligence has as to its imagined purpose. That device brought you here, and somehow I can't imagine you considering that a warlike act."

"What is it?" What's it doing here, then?"

"Aiding me occasionally. I'm merely an observer,"

said Dr. Nystrom. "I've been one for thirty years, on and off. An observer of people and events, mostly. I've been waiting—"

"For what?" Ross said, his suspicion still strong.

"For the time to arrive when I can discontinue my role and return home."

"Spy. Observer. Oh, what's the difference anyway?" Ross said, looking straight at him. "They both mean the same damn thing."

"Not at all, Ross. There is a difference in intent. I haven't made one aggressive move, and yet all I've encountered is suspicion and hostility here."

That was obviously true, Ross was forced to admit. Still doubts lingered. "Just who are you observing for, then?" Ross asked insistently. "Or more to the point—where is home for you?"

Dr. Nystrom went to a bookshelf and selected an astronomy text. He flipped through a diagram of the Milky Way, and where the stars were bunched together thickest he jabbed his finger down.

"There," he said.

Their world was not like Earth. It circled a huge star, an aging red giant, in the center of the galaxy, and it was a terrifying, merciless planet. They lived in clusters of dwellings scattered over the face of their world, separated by seemingly impassable rifts and chasms in the planetary crust. Dust storms roared unceasingly across the nightmare landscape.

Early in their history they abandoned the concept of vehicular travel, turning instead to *portals,* energy fields capable of weakening the fabric of space at selected points and then joining them to form instantaneous passageways. Using the *portals,* no place is more than a single footstep from another. For millions of years they perfected the intricacies of controlling the *portal* fields.

Their solitary history began to weigh heavily, and so they extended their chain of *portals* to the other planets of their solar system. They were all barren, lifeless.

Possessed by the desire to explore, the *portal* fields were pushed further, crossing the breach of space to the nearest star where more disappointments awaited. The next star, then the next were reached. The *portal* web expanded relentlessly outward, leaping from sun to sun, out toward the rim of the galaxy. From star to star they searched for the signs of life, and finding none, they drove on, thinking surely the planets of the next sun would be inhabited. But arrival found only the clouds and rocks and seas of a million other worlds.

The searching grew more frantic and desperate, racing across the deeps between the stars. They were growing anxious and weary. Could the entire galaxy be devoid of life?

A line of *portals* was strung down one of the spiral arms of the galactic wheel. They found a common yellow sun, nine planets, one of them a blue-green world called Earth by the intelligent creatures crowding its land masses. After centuries of fruitless searching, the shock of contact was enormous and the searchers withdrew in haste. They reapproached with great caution. Patiently, they studied the new world from afar. Then, with great caution, they began to send disguised observers into the mainstream of life on Earth to watch and listen and remember.

A sharp *ping!* sounded from the alien device in the wall, interrupting Dr. Nystrom's narrative, and Ross realized that it must have something to do with controlling the *portal* field. It sounded again. Dr. Nystrom's hand jerked in the middle of an expansive gesture when he heard it a third time.

"Pardon me," he said, and hurried over to the portal control with a worried expression on his face.

Ross was only partially aware of the *portal's* signaling. Most of his thoughts concentrated on the implications of what he had just heard. Dr. Nystrom's account of his people's expansion through the galaxy had left Ross not a little shaken and afraid, and started him wondering seriously how he and everyone else fit into the master plan slowly being revealed to him. He knew now, for certain that all their lives would be in some manner altered by the train of events that had led to this meeting in this room. How painful the adjustments to come might be Ross did not care to speculate. He was sure they wouldn't come easily.

Once again, he thought, humankind is at the crossroads. Deep within him, he felt a chill at the thought. He could not rid himself of strong doubts about the ability of people to handle such a massive decision. The record of history was far from encouraging. Ross was thinking of Eva Keough in particular.

There was another *ping!* as if to underscore her presence. Dr. Nystrom had already activated a screen on the *portal* controls; marked in a simple grid pattern, it was clear but for a single red dot advancing toward the middle.

Dr. Nystrom tapped his forefinger on the crimson speck in an erratic beat.

"That light represents the position of the warship, Ross," he said with some agitation evident in his voice. "It has come hunting for us."

CHAPTER EIGHTEEN

The warship itself appeared as a bright star moving among a string of equally bright stars, but there was no mistaking its existence. An incandescent exhaust flare trailed behind it, a spear of light flung back across the darkness.

"It's maneuvering into a parallel orbit," said Dr. Nystrom, after a moment at the grid screen. "I wonder if I can pick up its frequency—"

While he went over to the controls of his radio receivers, Ross centered his attention on the image in the screen.

At a distance of two hundred miles, the machine seemed to be a spider suspended in space. Ross found he could discern some details of the ship: the radiating fins stretching out like legs, the crew module like a round head where clusters of cabin lights burned carelessly, arrogantly.

It was plain, Ross thought, that they felt that *Boreas* was not worth their taking even the most elementary steps against detection. They knew they could overwhelm the station with about zero effort. It was like a battleship preparing to fight a lighthouse: no contest. The battleship's commander wouldn't be sweating the outcome.

As though he were reading Ross's thoughts at that moment, Dr. Nystrom said, "If you want out, say the word. They will probably begin the attack soon, and it's entirely possible there may be no prior warning."

"I'm thinking about it," Ross replied. "You know *Boreas* is a sitting duck, don't you? Just the same as relay satellite. Only there weren't any people aboard the relay when it got burned."

"That's correct. And that is also my point, Ross. The relay never had a chance. It couldn't survive because it couldn't think. It was only a machine. *Boreas* is different, because as long as I stay aboard, I can think for it."

"Both of us should leave," Ross said insistently.

"As I said before, Ross, if you want to go, tell me."

"But you're not?"

"Obviously not."

Obvious it was. Dr. Nystrom returned to his work, pointedly ignoring the menacing shape hovering out there. Why was he doing it? Why was this station so important? And more, why was Earth so important to one whose own society—he had just admitted—had access to nothing less than all the stars, a way to reach the entire galaxy, unhampered by the speed of light? What extraordinary beings Nystrom's race must be, Ross thought, they must be on the order of gods! And then Ross smiled, remembering the stories of the Greek gods who somehow were fascinated with the affairs of men and liked nothing better than a little meddling with mortals. The outcomes of those mythical intrusions rarely were happy. But that was legend.

This was real. Men and aliens were coming to a confrontation, and there would be disaster whichever side won. Surely, Ross thought, if Eva Keough's ship wrecked the *portal* and killed Dr. Nystrom there would be unimaginable reprisals from the stars, and just as surely proud Earth never would accept defeat peacefully. Too many monster films had demonstrated that clearly enough.

There had to be another solution, he thought with rising panic. Ross was fully aware that if he helped Dr. Nystrom he would be considered a traitor in the hearts of every single human being on Earth; it would be a betrayal of the first magnitude. And yet, he could not leave Dr. Nystrom on *Boreas* alone. He would not betray his own conscience.

"I've made up my mind," he told Dr. Nystrom. "I'm staying. What can we do?"

"I have been trying to open a communications link with the ship, but there's been no reply. We'll have to let them make the first move."

The warship already was moving. With its primary drive turned off, it revolved slowly, and Ross could see hatches begin to slide back as antennae poked from portions of the hull. He peered closer.

"They're extending a long strut from the bow," said Ross.

"I know," replied Dr. Nystrom. "I've directed one of the *portal's* viewing screens on it."

Crossing the laboratory in a single motion of his arms, Ross braked to a halt on the opposite wall beside Dr. Nystrom. The *portal* screen showed the strut far more clearly, and Dr. Nystrom boosted the magnification several degrees. The strut appeared to leap closer until its tip filled the screen entirely. A bulbous device seemed to be pointed directly at the screen.

"There's the laser," said Dr. Nystrom. "Better get back into your suit, Ross. The atmosphere in this room will vent into space the first time the station wall is punctured."

"What about the lights?" Ross was struggling with his suit's backpack, then secured his helmet to its adaptor, switched on the low-power UHF suit radio and anxiously checked his supply of oxygen. The tank level read out a full three-quarters of an hour. As he watched, the wrist counter dropped from *45 min.* to *44 min.* Then he heard the radio come on.

"The lighting can withstand an air loss," said Dr. Nystrom. "They're tied into the main line from the reactor. So's the *portal.*"

In silence, they watched the vision screen. The ship retracted several of its probes and sensing devices, and

167

extended other objects that unfolded like metal flowers greeting the sun. Ross discovered that it was easy to forget that the ship was an artificial creation, for with every movement it seemed to gather life within it and prepare to wriggle free of its pupa and emerge to dry itself in the cold starlight.

The ship extended a dish antenna and pointed it in their direction.

"*Boreas* station," the radio speaker crackled. "Come in, Dr. Alfred Nystrom. We know you are aboard because we have been monitoring the carrier signals from your suit radios."

"This is Dr. Nystrom," Ross heard. "I assume this is Commander Keough, so let's skip the formalities. What do you want?"

"Dr. Nystrom! Such naïveté," she returned, sounding as though she were scolding an irresponsible child. "You will surrender yourself and stand trial on charges of espionage at a later—"

"No." That was all, but Ross could sense the cold anger and determination in his voice.

"I must caution you, Dr. Nystrom, that your—what is the proper term?—your unique status will not avail you in the least."

"I'm not sure I follow you," Dr. Nystrom replied.

"Don't attempt to evade the issue," Commander Keough said savagely. Then she seemed to realize her mistake, and her voice returned to its usual tone. "There is no more time for pretenses. I believe that you have not grasped the situation fully. Let me explain it for you. The little spy ring you constructed is now entirely broken up, Dr. Nystrom. One of its members is dead, the other has confessed to everything, *everything*. We know precisely what you are and, thanks to Dr. Ahn, we also have an excellent description of your operation."

"Then you can see that there is no need for force," replied Dr. Nystrom immediately.

"On the contrary. I see every reason for it at this

168

point, and I am prepared to use it if you don't surrender."

Dr. Nystrom covered his radio mike with his hand and turned to Ross, saying, "If Dr. Ahn actually did 'confess,' then they may have learned about the *portal.*"

"That's exactly what I was thinking," Ross said. "You might be able to use it as a bargaining tool."

"Perhaps, but I'm a bit worried about letting it fall into their hands. No, I don't see any other way out of this situation." He uncovered the microphone and said, "My decision stands. I'm not going to surrender either myself or the station."

"You are painting yourself into a tight corner. Well, then, what about you, Mr. Moran? I should tell you I have United Nations authorization to destroy *Boreas* station if I deem it necessary."

Ross had been hoping to avoid the interchange between the ship and the station, but now he was committed—one way or the other—by his next words.

"I agree with Dr. Nystrom," Ross found himself saying.

"That is most unfortunate. I had hoped you would see your way clear of this matter and choose the right course."

"I have."

He tried to say more, but he heard a distinct *click* as the ship's UHF transmitter was switched off angrily. Looking into the view screen he saw the laser swing around on its strut and glow redly.

It fired a single intense burst of light that struck the station off to one side. The glow faded while the laser cycled through a brief cooling period, then fired again. This time their aim had improved.

A furiously bubbling hole appeared in the lab wall.

Instantly it had burned through and was blazing on the opposite bulkhead.

The room air screamed out into space.

The laser cycled. And fired again.

Another white-hot patch seared the cabin close to the

169

portal controls. Ross shouted to Dr. Nystrom as the metal softened, then splattered across the lab, a stinging molten nebula.

The laser cycled, cooling its components. . . .

The next round struck only a bare two-and-a-half feet from Dr. Nystrom who ducked away. He said hoarsely, "They must be using an advanced sensing device to aim that laser, Ross."

Ross nodded, seeing the line of punctures snaking toward the *portal*.

The laser fired and cycled. And fired and cycled. And fired and cycled. It was an insistent hypnotic rhythm that never broke tempo. never stopped. Fire and cycle. And fire and cycle. And fire . . .

A wild shot grazed Dr. Nystrom's suit, burning across his chest while he froze and watched the fire flay the cloth an inch from his skin. It continued onward, smashing the lights into glass fragments and powder.

"We have to fight back," Ross said.

"There is no way," replied Dr. Nystrom, his voice sounding dead and defeated. *"Boreas* is unarmed."

"There's the *portal*," Ross told him. An idea was forming, and Ross started for the lab door as a bolt of light slashed past his eyes and crisped the hinges. In a moment they were slag.

Zero gravity helped him as he flung himself down the hallway outside the laboratory. At the end was the emergency station; Ross grabbed the fireaxe and started back.

Laserfire riddled the lab now, carving hunks of wall and machinery. But it hadn't yet reached the *portal* controls, and Ross prayed for a few more seconds.

Dr. Nystrom stared uncomprehendingly at the axe Ross held.

Ross said urgently, "Warm up the *portal* and set it to move me next to the ship's laser. I'll take a crack at it with this blunt instrument." Ross shook the axe vigorously.

Dr. Nystrom stared at him, his eyes widening. Then

he chuckled lightly and turned to the controls, swiftly setting up the *portal* despite the flashes of light narrowing around him.

"Well, it's ready," he told Ross, and reached for the switch. Ross steeled himself, preparing for the shock. It never came.

"Ross," said Dr. Nystrom. "I can't! There's no gravity out there, nothing to brace against. If you tried to heft the axe, you'd spin toes-over-teakettle in the opposite direction."

Action and reaction: Newton's third law.

"I get the picture, thanks." He paused, dismayed, seeing the *portal* now fully alive, waiting. For nothing. And then again . . .

Ross straightened himself confidently. "Why not turn the idea around? Move the laser *in here.*"

"Into the lab?" replied Dr. Nystrom in a quavering voice. "It would mean shifting the mass-exchange balances to compensate for the increase in power drain." He went to the controls again.

Two hundred miles away, the spaceship fired.

The station walls were giving way under the intense heat. Through a rent in the wreckage, Ross caught a worried glimpse of their antagonist—a deadly bright speck among the stars.

"The *portal's* focused directly on the laser," Dr. Nystrom announced. "Find yourself a good handhold, Ross."

Ross jammed his booted feet under a buckled steel bar that had sprung loose from the computer console support. When he had wedged himself in tight enough, Ross nodded.

Dr. Nystrom triggered the *portal,* Ross felt a vestige of tension grip him as—in some process he could not even begin to comprehend—the fabric of space was ruptured. This room and the tip of the laser spar were fusing into a single continuous niche in the structure of the universe. Ross swung the axe.

In the center of the lab, the laser flickered into existence, a convolution of mirror-polished components,

171

glittering in the unsteady light. Awkwardly the fireaxe crashed into it. He felt the handle twist from his fingers.

"Ross, get back!" Dr. Nystrom yelled at him.

The laser shimmered.

And the *portal* reversed itself. The fabric of space unwound, springing back to normality, restoring order to the universe and returning the laser.

Ross and Dr. Nystrom crowded around the screen. There, on the bow of the warship, stood the laser, intact. Ross felt his heart sink miserably, thinking, it's all the same!

Dr. Nystrom stepped up the magnification, and they both saw it. The axehandle was deeply embedded in the laser, and in a moment it had been withdrawn into the hull of the ship.

Not long after, they heard a transmission beamed their way. "Very nice indeed, Dr. Nystrom. I haven't decided how you accomplished that, and I suspect that your Dr. Ahn was holding out some important details on us, but actually it is of little importance. We came prepared for surprises: your sleight-of-hand won't keep you alive forever. I have just received instructions to extend a final opportunity to you. You must surrender."

"Commander," said Dr. Nystrom, "this is all a complex matter. Perhaps we can compromise on a few points?"

"Not at all. This is an ultimatum," Eva Keough said. "Also, I would be derelict in my duty if I permitted myself to be taken in by your assurances. I have an unpleasant idea of what a 'compromise' would entail."

There was no warning. Three small missiles came hurtling toward *Boreas,* traveling far faster than Dr. Nystrom could anticipate. "I can't keep them in focus," he cried.

They impacted simultaneously. One exploded into the supply dock, another plowed into the rotating gravity section of the station and detonated with a dull rumble. The third went wide of its mark, missing the radio astronomy lab entirely. It smashed against a parabolic antenna, broke in two, and then struck the nuclear reactor.

The lab rattled. When Ross looked up, he could see only the blackened stump; the reactor itself was scattered for miles in every direction.

Tossed from his place by the *portal* controls, Dr. Nystrom flailed his arms helplessly in the dark lab before he collided with a stray cable. He grabbed for it and pulled himself back to the controls and tried a few adjustments. But Ross could see that the effort was hopeless. The *portal* was dead, not one of the indicators lighted now that the power source had been destroyed. *Boreas* station was defenseless. Worse, there was no means of retreat; they were trapped.

Strangely, this line of thought seemed not to have occurred to Dr. Nystrom. He was disassembling the *portal* control housing, and soon his head and arms were poked into a servicing compartment. Then Ross saw the pulsing flashes of a microtorch at work.

It was all so futile. "Dr. Nystrom," said Ross slowly, "you might as well forget it. I just had a glimpse outside. That missile barrage wiped out the reactor for keeps."

"I realized that when the *portal* quit on me," came the reply. "And I was afraid they'd shot out the fuel cells, too. But they missed. I'm crossing over the leads."

The torch guttered out, and Dr. Nystrom moved back. Already the indicators were blinking on, one by one, across the panel.

"Ah, that's better," said Dr. Nystrom. He turned to Ross. "In a moment the warship will realize *Boreas* survived, and they will finish their work. So I'm going to send you to Earth using the *portal*."

"That sounds sensible. And you'll follow me, right?"

Dr. Nystrom shook his head. "I can't chance Eva Keough capturing the *portal*," he said with a quavering voice. "That would be—utterly unthinkable."

"But it would be even worse if you don't use the *portal* yourself. You're the only one who can stop what's happening by explaining that you don't represent a threat to Earth. I believe it, but nobody else has seen what I have. They won't know what the truth is, Dr. Nystrom, unless you tell them yourself!"

Ross picked his way through the shambles of the radio astronomy lab to a place where a corner of the room had been torn away. He looked out.

Nearly the entire station had been demolished. The supply dock was crumpled up like foil against the front of *Boreas,* its landing-approach radars were bent at a dozen angles. Everywhere the outer plating was peeled back, revealing layers of rubble beneath, and in the exact center of the gravity section a hole had been blasted completely through. It was large enough for a space tug to pass through without bumping the sides of the tunnel. Wherever Ross turned his eyes he saw the ruins of familiar things like a window burned to lumps of glass, or a bottle that had exploded its contents out into space.

"There's sufficient wattage in the fuel cells for the *portal* to make one more transfer," said Dr. Nystrom. "It is very feeble. I doubt it could reach the Centauri system, and the range might be far less, maybe only the solar system itself, therefore, you must consider leaving *Boreas.*"

Ross would have replied, but his attention was drawn to the viewer. There, the ship had launched a massive object, far larger than the missiles. It floated freely for a second, then a jet of fire started it moving ponderously toward the station.

"I think you'd better concentrate on *that*. It's their knockout punch," Ross guessed aloud. A thermonuclear punch.

The bomb slowly gathered momentum, but Dr. Nystrom had no problem focusing the *portal* on it. He easily locked the controls onto the weapon.

It started to accelerate now.

The *portal* indicators were bright, ready, but Dr. Nystrom hesitated over the switches that would snap away the weapon.

"What's the matter?" asked Ross anxiously. The

bomb was halfway to the station, and Dr. Nystrom's hand had not moved. He saw that the ship was backing away from its previous position. Must be some kind of bomb, Ross thought, if they're scared of it, too.

Even through the transparent faceplate of his suit, Ross could see the weapon closing on them. "Dr. Nystrom!"

Dr. Nystrom seemed paralyzed. His hand hung over the *portal*, rigid as a metal rod.

The bomb traced a flat arc from the point of launch toward *Boreas* station. Its single rocket engine labored to overcome the initial resistance, but soon the projectile was away from the warship and streaking across the gap of space. In the final seconds it enlarged and swelled to the edges of the view screen. The remaining half-dozen miles separating it from the station flashed by.

Ross could not discern whether Dr. Nystrom had moved in that last rushing moment.

The projectile drove on, as long and wide and massive as a monorail coach, blunt and ugly. It was yards distant, then feet, and then inches.

Ross dragged his gaze aside from the screen. From the corner of one eye he imagined he saw a flicker of motion in the lab. Something was moving again and again. Dr. Nystrom was collapsing across the *portal* controls, his gloved hand spasmodically depressing the activating plate over and over.

The *portal* was a lifeless blank. The energies that powered it were already expended. No indicator lights showed, and the view screen was a featureless rectangle.

Ross's movement continued to swing him around until he was staring out beyond the demolished walls of the station, out into space where the pale hemisphere of the moon hung.

The lunar darkside was pierced by a fireball as intense as the sun as the hydrogen bomb detonated a few miles above a low ringwall crater. A dome of light washed over the surface of the moon, and for one instant the entire sphere was bathed in incandescence.

This event, Ross thought, was a unique moment in the flow of history; since the creation of the solar system there had been no precedent for this spectacular display of power. He stood transfixed at the incredible sight until the nuclear glow subsided and darkness came ebbing back.

Three hundred miles from the station, the warship kept to its position.

Dr. Nystrom seemed to revive. "I imagine they will be radioing us shortly," he said and looked sorrowfully around. "Let's see what can be done to repair the *portal*."

That precaution proved unnecessary, for soon radio contact was opened by Eva Keough's resigned and defeated voice. Then she listened, subdued and solicitous, when Dr. Nystrom stated his terms to her. The exchange was completed in a minute.

The battle for *Boreas* station was over. Just beginning, however, was the far wider struggle for the destiny of all the men and women of Earth.

CHAPTER NINETEEN

The wardroom was located directly amidships of the spherical forward module. The architects and engineers who had secretly drawn up the blueprints for the warship had designed the room so that it could be quickly converted into a general meeting area. But it was clearly evident that they had not foreseen this gathering, or they would have tripled the dimensions of the floor and included a great many more chairs.

The wardroom, now an auditorium, was packed tight, mostly with faces unfamiliar to Ross. There were scores of officials in evidence: Committeemen from the UN, ISA functionaries, and many others. A shuttle flight up from Main Station had just arrived and was discharging a dozen bewildered-looking diplomats who, Ross imagined, would be even unhappier when they discovered all the available chairs and benches had been claimed by earlier arrivals. They would have to be contented with boxes and crates, or the cold steel floor.

Altogether there had been nine shuttles run here in the few hours since the battle for *Boreas* station, and several more were scheduled to dock at the warship's landing stage before the assembly Dr. Nystrom had called would get underway. Only one shuttle was returning to Main Station; all the pilots, it appeared, were as interested in Dr. Nystrom's upcoming remarks as the statesmen they had ferried here.

Ross waited for the meeting to open with ill-concealed impatience.

He had just come back to the wardroom from the landing stage, after seeing Myra and Joel Colbert off in the Main Station-bound shuttle. They had been been held as the unwilling "guests" of Eva Keough since the forcible evacuation of *Boreas* half a day ago and the collective strain had been telling on both of them. They had gladly accepted seats on the departing shuttle to Main, despite their desire to see what their old and surprising friend, Dr. Nystrom, was up to.

And, apparently, everyone else wanted to know also. Predictably, Dr. Nystrom was the number one topic of discussion, comment, and rumor. The latter was most prevalent, since he refused to discuss his plans with anyone, even Ross. Ross felt his own knowledge was so limited and fragmentary it would only aggravate the wild rumors being passed around the room if he revealed what he knew.

He was fast becoming bored with the illustrious and famous national leaders seated everywhere around him. Their presence was enervating and disappointing, since they alternated their conversation between petty domestic chatter and the most foolish speculation he had ever heard. They were, he realized in dismay, exactly mirroring the rest of humanity.

These dismal thoughts were swept away a moment later.

Dr. Nystrom strode confidently into the room.

He was trailed by murmurs of nervous applause and whispering. Many bent forward to have a better look at him, since it was said he was a very unusual individual.

He began by relating the history of his own race, in the same manner he had described it to Ross on the eve of the battle. First he spoke of his world's hostile environment, and then linked it to the evolution of the space-bridging *portals*.

After pausing to detail the operations of the *portal's*

energy fields, Dr. Nystrom explained the movement of his people out into galactic space in their frantic hunt for companion life-forms among the multitude of stars that ended with the discovery of Earth.

Ross noticed that Dr. Nystrom seemed to be at the peak of his form, his voice was vibrant and resoundingly clear, his body showed no signs of tenseness or fatigue. In all he seemed incredibly alert and fit considering all that he had undergone. That alone, Ross was thinking, probably impressed the assembly of delegates more than any technical description of the *portal*. After all, they had already *seen* the dramatic power of that device.

As before, Ross found himself irresistibly drawn into the story Dr. Nystrom was weaving; for he found that Dr. Nystrom was not merely repeating the facts he had given Ross previously, but was enlarging on the bare outline. Ross was most fascinated by his disclosure that an individual of his own race had a lifetime far longer and different than a human's.

"For example," Dr. Nystrom said, "I am considered a relative youngster by my race, but I am already several centuries older than the eldest of you in this room."

That caused a considerable stir in the room. Dr. Nystrom was content to allow it to continue awhile. When at last the mass of officials and delegates quieted, they discovered Dr. Nystrom had taken a wholly new tack.

He taped a wall map of the world onto the back partition and pointed to the Australian subcontinent before he spoke again.

"A senseless and destructive war is about to be fought to take possession of that region of Earth," Dr. Nystrom said. "It will occur because another nation has become too crowded to feed and shelter its own people. The solution, they think, is emigration to Australia. The Australians don't see eye-to-eye, and are prepared to fight to keep them out.

"We know that the war will be a disaster. It will settle nothing because of the nature of the problem,

179

the implacably rising numbers will eventually cancel out any gains made, and then another war will be brewing. Everywhere on Earth this same cycle continues, out of control. There exist no new empty lands to which men can move in times of trouble. The age of exploration ended centuries ago, and now all the habitable continents are claimed and occupied. The moon and the planets of the solar system cannot support human life, and the stars are so distant that even a spaceship as advanced as this one," he said with a sweep of his hand, "would require a hundred years to make a one-way trip."

He let his hand drop. Ross heard a grumbling acknowledgment of Dr. Nystrom's theme from the audience. They were all too well aware of the conditions in each of their countries; they knew about the hunger and the homelessness and the gnawing despair that afflicted the seven billion over all of Earth.

"Perhaps," Dr. Nystrom began, "you now understand how these ideas dovetail.

"My own race is long-lived, and our numbers are comparatively few. It was a comfortable situation while we were restricted to our native world, but completely insufficient to even begin to truly explore and settle the galaxy. For us, there are a billion new planets suddenly opened up, and not enough individuals to accomplish more than a rapid survey of one before departing for another.

"On the other hand, Earth has far too many people. Your civilization is crumbling slowly because their needs cannot be met."

One of the UN officials had gotten to his feet by this time.

"If I read you correctly," he said to Dr. Nystrom, "I think that you are proposing some sort of arrangement between your world and Earth?"

"Yes," Dr. Nystrom replied. "But I'll be more specific. I had in mind a partnership, right from the start, with the objective of exploring and colonizing the worlds that the *portal* has already revealed to us.

180

Thousands more, we are sure, are suitable, and only waiting for the survey teams to find them."

"Just what do you mean, suitable worlds?"

"Planets much the same as Earth. Where people can settle without the need for elaborate life-support machinery."

Another official had stood up. "Do you honestly think anyone will voluntarily walk into one of your— your *portals* only to be flung off who knows where? Some faraway desert or jungle?"

"It will require courage. But the cities of Earth are jungles themselves at this moment. I've walked the streets of Calcutta, Rio, Tokyo, and New York and often considered them far more dangerous than an uninhabited world."

"Many won't like it," the man continued. "They won't like to be told to leave."

"They will not have to," replied Dr. Nystrom. "Those who wish to remain, can. But there are plenty of restless souls who will go. For them this will be a chance to begin their lives over, to start again. And they'll take this opportunity, or my estimation of Earthmen is all wrong."

After that rejoinder, the audience fell into silence.

Finally an elderly diplomat rose and asked, "I have heard enough to convince myself, at least, that you are sincere. I find that after all you have explained, only one point has not been touched upon. It is this: you have extended an offer that truly is astronomical, and yet you have refrained from saying what you wish in return. Tell us now, what is the price?"

"There is no price in a partnership," said Dr. Nystrom. "Except mutual respect and a common trust."

Following the meeting, the delegates and officials split into enclaves to discuss the offer Dr. Nystrom had presented. Even the shuttle pilots, who were as much spectators at this awesome gathering as was Ross, went into a huddle of their own. Ross went over to Dr. Nystrom.

"Did you happen to hear what's being said?" said Dr. Nystrom eagerly. "I wonder what their reaction is."

"I think they agree with you," replied Ross. "In principle, at least."

"That's all I was hoping for. What is taking place now is only the barest of beginnings, of course; delegations from both our worlds will have to handle the details later on." He gave a faintly self-deprecating smile, and added, "After this, I refuse to get embroiled in interplanetary diplomacy!"

Before Ross could speak a messenger arrived and told both of them that Eva Keough had requested a few minutes to speak to them.

"There's time enough, I suppose," said Dr. Nystrom warily.

Ross was equally hesitant in his agreement. For he knew that Eva Keough had suffered one setback after another recently. First, the military had forced her resignation, then taken away her command of the warship. The ISA immediately confiscated the huge space vessel and placed her under arrest. She was being held in her cabin aboard her own ship, possibly the most humiliating circumstance that she had ever been subjected to. Ross felt sure these reversals had not improved her volatile nature, but his sense of curiosity got the better of him and he nodded.

The messenger led them along several branching corridors to a large door. The ISA had posted a brawny man to stand guard at the makeshift brig, but he was a pure formality. The spaceship itself was a tighter prison than any installation on the ground, since there was literally no place to which to escape. The guard stood aside and let them enter.

Eva Keough jumped suddenly when Dr. Nystrom closed the door behind him. Her hair in disarray and the immaculate black uniform that Ross remembered was now soiled and dusty, but her voice at first was calm and level.

"Now that you are here," she began, "there is something I wish for you to know. And that is—"

Then the deliberate control in which she held herself broke all at once.

"I—I want to offer my apologies," she blurted out, unrestrained by her usual poise. Emotion held her in a fist and squeezed out of her a torrent of stumbling regrets for her acts. Ross felt no sense of satisfaction hearing her, no triumphant sense of retribution, nothing at all but pity and a mocking hollowness that another person should be deprived of all their dignity now.

She turned away in silence.

"I will accept that," Dr. Nystrom said at last in a quiet, even tone.

"You will . . . but how can you" Her voice trembled, incredulous. "After everything you know—"

"It all lies in the past, and the past is dead and gone as far as I am concerned," Dr. Nystrom told her. "I am to blame for so much of the misunderstanding myself. My own concern for subterfuge, really, was the trigger for your reactions."

"I saw you as a threat—" she said awkwardly.

"—and responded to it. No one can fault you for that, given the conditions as they existed then," Dr. Nystrom said.

"Do you forgive that response, then?"

"No. I'm as tied up and as guilty as you are, so how can I forgive you? If events had been only a trifle different, I would be sitting where you are now, most likely, and putting the question to you," he said. There wasn't the slightest trace of rancor or reproof in his voice or expression.

Ross thought that here, for the first time, they were regarding one another in a new light, with a new kind of recognition. He thought, now they are seeing the basic similarities in themselves, and they understand. They are equals.

CHAPTER TWENTY

Two days later, Ross was having breakfast with Dr. Nystrom, Tim, and Christy in the little café on Main Station.

It began as a quiet, relaxed get-together, but soon developed into something quite different. By this time, Dr. Nystrom had become a prominent figure in the world press and something of a celebrity no matter how he tried to avoid the dubious distinction. He spent much of the meal shooing away reporters, cameramen, and autograph hunters.

Midway through, Ross could tell that Christy was fairly bubbling over with an announcement. The matter was soon put to rest when she proudly displayed an engagement ring that shone nearly as much as she did.

"Isn't it terrific?" she said happily. "Just imagine, he kept it in his pocket a whole year before he finally got around to asking." She gave Tim a playful nudge.

"Hey! Take it easy," he said. "What kind of doctor are you, anyway? Remember I'm a wounded man."

Christy returned an affectionate smile and remarked to Ross and Dr. Nystrom, "As soon as the battle-scarred hero recovers, we're moving on—to Sydney, Australia. That's going to be the first emigration terminal for Earth, once they get the *portal* transferred from *Boreas* and reassembled on solid ground."

Ross was grinning. "It really is a small universe. I

was just considering emigrating. Seriously. The colony worlds will be needing trained weather forecasters pretty soon, I imagine. And I've got an idea for forming an interplanetary weather service."

Tim looked blank. "You're putting me on. How can weather be interplanetary?"

"Dr. Nystrom's been telling me about some of the planets that are suitable for colonization, and it started me thinking. If the *portal* can transport men and materials from star to star, then it ought to be a simple matter to move weather around, too. Say, clouds full of rain that would otherwise fall unneeded—and probably unwanted—on a jungle-type of planet could be redirected to a dry, desert world for aiding irrigation."

Tim started to nod in agreement, his imagination obviously stimulated. "I'll bet you could turn around that process, too. Use the heat of the deserts to warm up arctic climates, to release water for agriculture. And then—"

"Hold on," Ross said. "Why don't we join forces?"

Tim stopped. "We can't, Ross. Not for a while, at least. When Christy said we were heading for Australia, she should have added that we're going to be working in the new ISA hospital there. When it's built, we'll be preparing emigrants for the colonial worlds. The ISA has us under contract for a year, but when it is over we'll hunt you up."

"Good enough," Ross said. "But fair warning, I expect to have a thriving concern by then, so don't come expecting a vacation!"

Christy was looking across the table at Dr. Nystrom, who was staring off into the distance. "Something amiss?" she asked.

"No," he replied shortly, "just planning the outline of a speech on exobiology I have to deliver to the chief medical officers of the ISA tomorrow in Los Angeles. I've hundreds of notes in my briefcase here, but really I don't know what I am going to say."

"How can that be?" she said wonderingly. "You're the resident expert on non-Earthly life forms."

Ross felt a quivering chill at her words. It happened each time that topic was brought up. Dr. Nystrom's origin. Ross found himself saying, "it is weird. All along I never suspected you weren't . . . weren't . . ."

"Weren't actually human?" prompted Dr. Nystrom, and smiled when Ross nodded in assent. "Well, in part I *am,* though you can imagine I did not begin my existence that way. My own race does bear a slight physical resemblance to Earthlings, but years of skillful plastic surgery were required to alter me into a reasonable duplicate of a human. And of course the same technique was used on the others—the ones you knew as Dr. Ahn and Jonathan Hanks."

"It's an incredible job," said Tim appreciatively. "I never had an inkling."

"You might have," replied Dr. Nystrom. "All the while there was a way—and that was my single greatest worry. You see, outside," he said, rubbing his face, "I look like plain old *homo sapiens;* my internal organs, though, are vastly different. Any surgeon who got me under the knife would have spotted me for what I am instantly."

"That never happened," Tim mused. "You were the healthiest man I ever met."

"A built-in precaution, I assure you. I took special pains to avoid situations that might expose me to risk of injury: but the others were always finding themselves in trouble."

Dr. Nystrom laughed in mild exasperation. "You would not believe the scrapes they wandered into! Dr. Ahn loved hiking in the wilds though he wasn't especially proficient at it. A couple of months ago he became lost in the woods inside Rocky Mountain National Park and I had to use the *portal* to rescue him before he froze—what's so funny about that, Tim?"

"Oh, I've just been exonerated from a charge of overactive imagination in the case of a singular odor," he replied blandly, shooting a gloating look at Ross.

"Private joke, eh?" said Dr. Nystrom, puzzled. "Later, when Hanks died in the Arctic, I knew that the doctor aboard that Russian submarine would perform an autopsy on him—it's required by international sea laws. That's when my masquerade was over. Finis! I had to rush to salvage what I could, after Military Intelligence finally put all the pieces together and arrested Dr. Ahn."

A uniformed flight attendant came over to the table. "Dr. Alfred Nystrom? Mr. Ross Moran?" he inquired. "Your shuttle is departing in ten minutes."

There were many reluctant goodbyes before Dr. Nystrom and Ross listlessly left the cafe for the hub of Main Station.

"Dr. Nystrom," Ross started to ask as they walked. He halted his train of thoughts. "Dr. Nystrom? What do I call you now, anyway? I'm so used to—you know—"

He answered with a shrug. "Why bother changing it? It is the phonetic equivalent of my previous name. Here's our flight."

A stewardess showed them to their seats. The cabin door shut solidly. In a few moments the shuttle began to inch forward toward launch.

Then, very abruptly, it slammed to a stop. Ross was pitched forward in his seat. He heard vague clanking noises and attempted to see out the thick round window what the trouble was. "The catapult's gone and snapped," Ross heard another passenger grumble, followed by an answering groan and, "That'll mean we're late."

The door opened again, and a familiar-appearing flight attendant scrambled inside, clutching a black briefcase.

The attendant came puffing up the aisle, glancing from side to side until he saw Dr. Nystrom. He handed the briefcase to him, saying, "Your friends in the restaurant say you forgot this."

Sheepishly, Dr. Nystrom accepted it. "Thanks," he said.

Ross glanced around the cabin and saw that every passenger in the shuttle had turned around in their seats and were now looking with amusement at the famous Dr. Alfred Nystrom's plight.

Right now, Ross thought, I will bet all I own that he would just as soon sink quietly through the carpeting rather than face those lightly amused expressions.

"How could I have forgotten this?—all my notes!" said Dr. Nystrom in a whisper.

As the shuttle got under way again, he slumped down in his seat in chagrin, muttering, "In times past I could rationalize these sort of lapses, by saying, *sorry about that, folks! I'm only human—*"

He slumped down further, and the last thing Ross heard him say was, "I don't expect that one's going to do me much good any longer."

ON SALE WHEREVER PAPERBACKS ARE SOLD
—or use this coupon to order directly from the publisher.

MYSTERY & SUSPENSE

IF YOU ENJOYED THIS BOOK, HERE ARE MORE PAPERBACKS JUST RIGHT FOR YOU..

Ngaio Marsh

N2986	A Man Lay Dead 95¢ £
N2994	The Nursing Home Murder 95¢ £
N3017	Vintage Murder 95¢ £
N3081	Tied Up in Tinsel 95¢ £
N3158	Hand In Glove 95¢ £
N3184	Death of A Fool 95¢ £
N3265	Death in A White Tie 95¢ £

Mabel Seeley

N3001	The Whispering Cup 95¢ ‡
N2853	The Whistling Shadow 95¢ ‡
N3053	The Chuckling Fingers 95¢ ‡
N3250	Eleven Came Back 95¢ ‡

Send to: PYRAMID PUBLICATIONS,
Dept. M.O., 9 Garden Street, Moonachie, N.J. 07074

NAME _____

ADDRESS _____

CITY _____

STATE _____ ZIP _____

I enclose $_____, which includes the total price of all books ordered plus 25¢ per book postage and handling if the total is less than $5.00. If my total order is $5.00 or more, I understand that Pyramid will pay all postage and handling.

Please note: A book you have ordered might not be available at this time. To expedite your order—and provide all of the "good reading" you want—we suggest that you allow us to make reasonable substitutions of books in the same category, and at the same price—only if necessary!
☐ Yes, you may substitute if necessary. ☐ No substitutions, please. No COD's or stamps. Please allow three to four weeks for delivery.

P-12

Free catalog of hundreds of your favorite books

Choose from hundreds of popular-priced books in your favorite categories and order them conveniently by mail. To receive your Pyramid Paperback Catalog, fill in the label below (use a ball point pen please) and mail to Pyramid...

PYRAMID PUBLICATIONS
Mail Order Department
9 Garden Street
Moonachie, New Jersey 07074

NAME_____

ADDRESS_____

CITY_____STATE_____

P-4   ZIP_____